DRIA BOND

Love Interrupted

First published by Three Pines Publications 2021

Copyright © 2021 by Dria Bond

All rights reserved. No part of this publication may be reproduced, stored or transmitted in any form or by any means, electronic, mechanical, photocopying, recording, scanning, or otherwise without written permission from the publisher. It is illegal to copy this book, post it to a website, or distribute it by any other means without permission.

This novel is entirely a work of fiction. The names, characters and incidents portrayed in it are the work of the author's imagination. Any resemblance to actual persons, living or dead, events or localities is entirely coincidental.

First edition

This book was professionally typeset on Reedsy.
Find out more at reedsy.com

Contents

Acknowledgement		iv
1	Chapter 1	1
2	Chapter 2	11
3	Chapter 3	18
4	Chapter 4	28
5	Chapter 5	35
6	Chapter 6	41
7	Chapter 7	49
8	Chapter 8	54
9	Chapter 9	58
10	Chapter 10	66
11	Chapter 11	75
12	Chapter 12	83
13	Chapter 13	93
14	Chapter 14	98
15	Chapter 15	108
About the Author		115

Acknowledgement

I wanted to take this time and give a huge thank you to my family. For giving me space and the time to get this book and thoughts out of my head to place them on paper. Thank you so much to my Writer's Group; Lelia E. Hart, Roe Braddy, and Kristi Tailor, for giving me inspiration and pushing me daily to finish. This is truly a dedication to your love, support, and encouragement. To the readers, that took the time out to read and give me your thoughts, you guys are amazing. Because any negative remarks could have easily trashed this whole project from jump. Much thanks!!

    Thank **YOU** to the reader and those that purchased this book. I am beyond grateful and I truly hope you enjoyed it! And if you did enjoy this book please, please, please, be sure to leave a review. Negative or positive I would love to hear your thoughts. And as I said before, Thank you!!!

One

Chapter 1

Traci

"Ladies and gentlemen, welcome to Donald Sangster International. Local time is 8:25 p.m. and the temperature is 82 degrees.

For your safety and comfort, please remain seated with your seat belt fastened until the Captain turns off the fasten seat belt sign. This will indicate that we have parked at the gate and that it is safe for you to move about the cabin. At this time, you may use your cellular phones if you wish. Please check around your seat for any personal belongings you may have brought on board with you, and please use caution when opening the overhead bins, as heavy articles may have shifted around during the flight.

If you require deplaning assistance, please remain in your seat until all other passengers have deplaned. One of our crew members will be pleased to assist you then.

On behalf of American Airlines and the entire crew, I'd like to thank you for joining us on this trip, and we are looking forward to seeing you on board again in the near future. Have a good evening and enjoy your stay in Montego Bay!"

It was late evening when I touched down at MBJ International. It seemed as if I had been traveling forever. Almost 9 hours from L.A. to Jamaica. A trip I hoped would be well worth it. A trip, even though for business, it was much needed. A much needed getaway from Trevor; my lying, manipulating cheater of an ex fiance.

Trevor and I had been together going on almost seven years. We met each other in college my sophomore year, his junior year.

It was midday, I had just finished my last class of the day. I passed him while walking through the quad. Trevor was the typical college jock. He was surrounded by a babbling bunch of groupies as I passed. I overheard them talking about how they admired the way he looked on the court and other groupie nonsense. He seemed the type to be intrigued by his fellow admirers. I couldn't care less. Walking by I must have dropped my keys out of my bag. I didn't even realize until I got to my car and began to look for them. As I panicked, Mr. All Pro showed up.

"Hey, I think you dropped these," he said as he extended his hand and passed me my keys.

"Thanks, I would have been lost trying to figure out where I misplaced them."

"Yeah, well, I'm glad I was the one to find them. Trevor, nice to meet you." He said while reaching out his hand. Humoring him, I played along as if I didn't know his name.

"Traci," I said, returning the gesture. "Nice meeting you as well and thank you for returning my keys." I continued to unlock my door and placed my things in the car. . He continued

Chapter 1

to stand there after I thought his grand gesture was over, giving me the impression that I was wrong. I paused, looked up at him and replied, "Well, um, Thanks again. Hope you have a nice day!" Assuming that he would get the hint and that would be the end of the conversation. But you know what they say, ***When you assume you make an ass out of you;*** guess I was the ass that day. Already in my car and ready to drive, Trevor was still standing there looking like a lovesick puppy.

Trevor leaned into my car door, trying to drum up a conversation, "I haven't seen you around, are you a freshman?"

Correcting him immediately, "Sophomore."

"Oh, my bad. I've just never seen you before. I thought I knew all the cute faces on campus."

"What are you, the welcoming committee?" Gesturing back to his band of groupies. "Something like that," he laughed.

"Well, I'm going to let you get back to that. Thanks again! And it was nice to meet you, Trevor." I rolled up my window and drove off.

It seemed that if Trevor was in his right mind, he would have gotten the hint and tried to stay clear of me. Especially after I was so rude to him after he came and saved the day. That's what I got for assuming again…

I never truly paid attention to him in school. My primary focus was on my studies, because I didn't need any distractions to derail me from my goals.

I had boyfriends in high school, but they were never anything serious. I guess you would say they were only something to pass the time.

My mom would always tell me '***Traci, you change men like you change draws!***' And I couldn't even lie, it was true. As soon as a guy did something that was displeasing, they were dismissed without a second thought or explanation. It was out with the old, in with the new.

Trevor and I attended Cal State L.A. I enrolled after I graduated high school and stay there long enough to receive my MBA. Trevor was a promising basketball star with dreams of going pro. His major was computer science and being an all-around ladies' man.

The next couple of months, he spent his time fighting for my attention. Trying hard to get me to notice him. He was used to girls crawling all over him. The fact that I dismissed him and showed him no interest, intrigued him. I refused to defer my dream by getting entangled in his mess of cheating, lies and basketball. The efforts he went through to peak my interest, was a challenge for him. A challenge he eventually won and landed me in his entanglement.

As I exited the plane, I grabbed my carry-on bag and belongings. It was funny that after that long flight I wasn't exhausted as I thought I would be. Instead, I was surprisingly energized and excited. Excited to see what Montego Bay offered. I needed to do something, but I couldn't go exploring without my homegirl, Nat. I had to wait until she arrived, that way I wouldn't feel so alone or get into anything by myself.

I walked down to baggage claim to retrieve the rest of my belongings, and figured that I would catch the shuttle to the hotel and grab a drink at the nearby bar. I'd hoped they had some kind of late-night entertainment available.

The drive to the hotel seemed to take forever. Landmarks and buildings seemed to have a great deal of distance between them, so it took us forever to get to our destination. When we finally arrived at the plush hotel I stopped and took it all in; it was beautiful. There were beaches and pools surrounded by

Chapter 1

tall palm trees and endless lounge chairs. It was a paradise ... a much needed paradise.

After I took my bags up to my room I returned to the lobby to get a drink. As I walked to the bar to order my drink, a friendly bartender greeted me, "Hey there Pretty Gal, what can I get ya?" and he placed a beverage napkin in front of me.

"I don't know, surprise me. It's been a long week and I need something sweet but strong, that tastes good."

"I have just the thang for dat, com'n right up!"

It mesmerized me how quickly he gathered all the ingredients, placed them into the shaker, did a little bar magic, and poured my drink into a rimmed glass with pineapple and orange garnish. Afraid the concoction would catch me off guard and be too strong, I sipped it slowly. Being cautious went out of the door because the drink was oh so tasty. I automatically knew this was one of those drinks that would cause you to do something you'd regent, or you'd make a fool of yourself, if you were to have too many. I wanted to forget the days prior, but I had to pace myself.

Jay

The first day of many, it would seem. Another trip, traveling for business. I had to do what I had to do, though. Anything that would further develop my brand. I had been working ever so diligently to make my business a household name. We were already well known in L.A., Atlanta, Dallas, Houston, and New York. Now was the time to expand the business further. A place where I could truly get away. A paradise that I could use for both business and pleasure.

My assistant, Lisa helped set everything up. She had been in contact with a company that handled the contracts, called the clients and planned the initial meetings. All I had to do was come in, give everything a once over and sign my name on the dotted line. That was exactly how I liked to get things done. Everything that needed to be completed had to be finished correctly.

This week had been a long one, with the endless meetings and traveling here and there. Since I had two days before the meeting, I was going to take a well deserved break… I had spent a good majority of my career taking care of everything. At this point, the business practically ran itself. What would a couple of weeks without me hurt?

I took a long walk on the beach and decided to grab a drink before heading to my room. When I arrived at the bar, I motioned for the bartender to place my order. "Rum and coke, please," I requested.

"Com'n up!"

I grabbed my drink and sipped while surveyed the area, and noticed a stunning woman sitting and drinking by herself at a nearby table. She was like no other woman I'd ever seen before. Caramel toned skin, with copper colored locs, full lips, and a nice physique; just gorgeous. She could not be here alone, it was impossible.

She had to be with someone!

I watched and waited for someone to approach her table and take away my opportunity to get to know this beautiful creature.

Traci

I grabbed a table not too far from the bar after getting my drink. As I sat I was caught up in the music; Lost in the rhythm, I didn't even realize someone was standing in my personal space.

"May I have this dance?" The tall figure motioned with his

Chapter 1

hand outstretched to get me out on the dance floor. I didn't realize that he was talking to me until I felt him close, as he stood there waiting for my response.

Breaking my trance, I looked up at him. Usually when a girl was asked to dance, or offered a drink, was rarely from someone attractive. You'd get Bad Limp Bubba, or Tongue Tied Tyrone. Never in my wildest dreams would I have imagined that I would have been staring back at a 6'2 brown-skinned, a man that had almond color eyes, wearing a white button up. He appeared cool, with the top couple of buttons opened, khaki shirt and tan loafers. This man was a tall glass of water that I wouldn't mind using to quench my thirst. It had been a while since I went out dancing. Trevor never had been much of a dancer. So, if this man would be the one to offer, I sure wasn't going to decline.

After a long stare into his dreamy eyes, I was snatched back into reality.

Well, he won't stand here all night with his hand out. Get the hell up and go dance with the man. He won't bite, but if he did, I would enjoy it; with his sexy ass.

I quickly took his hand, knowing that if I stayed any longer that I would regret having him wait. "Sure," I said, taking his hand and we made our way to the dance floor.

My hips swayed to the music as I proceeded to the middle of the crowd. Feeling the music run through me as it sent electric currents to every nerve of my body. That's what I got for indulging in whatever cocktail that was. I grooved and raised my hands in the air as the music touched my soul. It was as if I'd almost forgotten that I had a dance partner, at least until I realized the music slowed down. Then the space between us was nonexistent, he grabbed my waist pulling me into a slow whine session. I figured that it would be a good time to get the formalities out of the way and introduce ourselves. "Nice to meet you. My name is Traci," I announced over the bass of the music.

"Jay, and the pleasure is all mine."

Wanting him to continue the conversation, I asked, "Where are you from?"

"New York, originally."

Umm, a New Yorker. There was something about an east coast accent that instantly made me want to start taking my panties off.. "Wow, I've never met anyone from New York before. How do you like it?" I responded awkwardly. Trying to create small talk after consuming alcohol, wasn't always the best idea.

"I mean, it was alright, always nice to have a change of scenery."

It seemed as if the music got even slower. Jay spun me around so that my back was against his chest… His body hovered over my 5'5 frame, and I could feel his manhood pressed against my back. I don't know if it was the liquor or just hormones, but I could feel a dampening in between my thighs. He reached down and whispered in my ear, "So what brings you to Jamaica?"

"A business vacay brought me here, but I'm out because I needed a break."

"Understood, I am here on business as well."

Jay smelled so good. It was as if I was in a trance. As the song ended, I broke the space between us to make sure I didn't give into temptation, I had to dismiss myself. "Hey, it was nice meeting you, Jay. Hope you enjoy your stay."

"Leaving so early?" He grabbed my hand as I tried to lead myself away from the alcohol fueled lust that was ever so strong between us. "The night's just getting started. Wouldn't you

Chapter 1

rather spend your night with good company than be alone?"

Jay had a point, and it left me speechless. Before I had a chance to respond, my body spoke up for me, leading me right back into his arms. For us to be participating in something as innocent as dancing, it only took an instant for my body to respond. To my surprise, I was as wet as an overflowing pool.

It had been over six months since the man that I thought I was gonna marry betrayed me and over a year since I had some. My body craved attention and fulfillment was in its grasp.

Jay broke the silence between us, "I hope it won't seem too forward of me, but would you like to join me for a night cap?"

Too forward, please.

I didn't want to seem too "forward" by letting him know that I wanted the same thing. It certainly wasn't my intention to come off like some kind of hoe, but after I thought about it, I realized it wasn't that serious. Hell, it's Jamaica, I live in L.A. I would probably never see him again. What happens in Jamaica, stays in Jamaica, right? I was on vacation and my body needed it.

"Not too forward at all, I would love to. That way we can get to know each other better without the noise," I responded. *Who was I kidding?* I hoped when we got to his room, that we would barely speak at all. Hopefully we'd let our bodies communicate without the presence of words. Unless the words ended in oohs and aahs. A million and one thoughts ran through my mind as we made our way to his room. I was nervous; it was almost like I was a virgin about to get deflowered. I had only had sex with the same man for the last seven years, plus I hadn't t had sex in over a year. My coochie had probably shriveled up to its original state. Them being called Cobweb Coochie, would have been an understatement.

The walk to his room seemed as if we were moving in slow motion, and took longer than I expected. Once we made it to the room, I realized I was sweating like a sinner in church. I was nervous that I was going to have to pay for the sins I thought we were going to commit behind the walls of his room. I secretly asked God if he was going to punish me, that he did so after everything was said and done. Maybe it was the alcohol or my hormones that had my imagination running wild. I had gotten ahead of myself. Perhaps Jay only had honorable intentions and only wanted to talk and get to know me better. Only time would tell.

Two

Chapter 2

Jay

When I saw her at the bar, I knew that I just had to have her. There was just something about her. Her vibe, her style, her demeanor. I wanted her to spread eagle across my bed, in my arms, while I fucked her. There was something about her that made my inner beast present himself, and wanting to rip away her clothes to have my way with her. But things like this had to be done with finesse. I took a deep breath, calmed my nerves and led her into my room.

"Would you like anything to drink?" I offered as she sat down in a nearby chair.

"I'll take a water, thank you! I think I'm done with any alcohol for the moment. Time to rehydrate."

I grabbed her water and myself another rum and coke from the mini fridge. I handed the drink to her as I took a seat beside her.

"I see you went all out, huh?" she commented about my room.

"I was trying to have the complete experience. You only live once right."

"You're absolutely right!" she agreed.

"So what brings you here to Jamaica?"

"Business and a much-needed break."."

"You're on the run?" I said with a light chuckle.

"I guess you could say that. On the run from my problems and past relationship." "I'm sorry that he hurt you."

"No need to apologize. You live and you learn. But how did you know that I was the one hurt and it wasn't the other way around?"

"When a woman hurts, she tries to find herself. Tries to find answers and reasons why. She also tries to get away from everything that would remind her of the past. It's the only way to clear her head. I presumed you lived with him, as well."

"Yes, unfortunately," she agreed disappointedly.

"Yes, see, more of a reason to run."

"And what are you, some kind of psychic?"

"No, I just grew up around a lot of women. My mom raised me right. She taught me how to treat a woman, how to please a woman, and to know what she needs before she even needs it."

"Oh, yeah? So tell me, what is it I need?"

"You need a man to treat you like none of the others you had in the past. To put you first *always*, not just when he feels the need to. To listen to you and feed your ambition. Am I close?"

She shifted in her chair as if my words hit her spot. Her body confirmed what I said to be true before her mouth could find the words. She let out a sigh.

"How do you—" I place my finger on her lips. Letting her know there was no need for any further conversation or

Chapter 2

explanation. Taking her by the hand, I led her to the bed.

Traci

Jay asked me to undress and lay face-down on the bed. He left the room, giving me privacy to disrobe and get under the sheet.

With my head down, cradled between my arms, my eyes closed, I slipped away into the back corners of my mind. I drifted off to another world. Leaving my senses with an acute awareness of his body, his touch. It was as if it was some kind of deep meditation.

I heard footsteps and felt his presence as he came back toward me. My heart beat faster. Making it hard to resume the deep dreamlike relaxed state I was in before.

I could smell the scent of his cologne. It smelled of a woodsy musk, leaving me even more open than I was before.

Jay stood near the bed, dimming the lights, rubbing oils between his hands. I could feel his heat as he moved closer to me. Jay worked his hand across my back, bringing me to a calming pleasure that directly sent a sensation to my lower region.

I was strongly attracted to him and I knew my body revealed it.

Jay

Working over her body, my hands served as my eyes. Removing the sheet to focus on her lower back and glutes, my palm traced her figure as I drew a more vivid picture of the rest of her in my mind. As my thumbs dug into her calves, legs and inner thighs, I imagined the pieces as a whole, standing nude in the dim light. I enjoyed the picture my hands created.

I worked until I reached to her upper back, leaned forward, digging my elbow into her as I positioned myself near her head. I kneaded my fingertips into her neck and shoulders. She was so tense, and I understood why. She was a woman in pain, longing for love, attention. Attention that I was willing to give to her, even if only for one night.

Thirty minutes into the rub down I requested, "Scoot down for me and turn on your back." I lifted the sheet to make it easier for her to maneuver. When she moved, I could tell that it aroused her, I let the sheet back down. Her honey pot released her nectar, as her lady parts glistened as if it was a diamond shining in the darkness. I grinned. I think I'm in love. I reached for the sheets and covered her up.

Her embarrassment was obvious as she closed her eyes completely to avoid our eyes meeting. At that moment, I could feel my own nature rise. The beast had officially been awakened.

Traci

Butterflies found their way from my chest to the place below my navel. I wanted him. I found that, for the first time in my life, without kissing, without foreplay, I was aroused. The last thirty minutes was all the preparation I needed. I wanted him right then and there. I refused to let this moment pass without getting a piece of him.

Lying there, juices flowing from my love box to my back, and heart in my throat, I felt vulnerable. He stepped away from the bed for a moment, and I was unsure of where he had gone. He started at my feet, caressing them gently leading up to my thighs. Spread my legs open, revealing my wetness. I reached for his hand, guiding it to my flower. Not knowing what to expect next, waiting in anticipation. Before I knew it, his fingers made

Chapter 2

their way inside me.

Mmm, how I loved a man that knew how to take charge!

He thrust in and out, working his magic, playing with my clit and penetrating my G-Spot. He played with it, giving me pleasurable torture, inserting yet another finger. I moaned in euphoric ecstasy. Unable to control myself, I let out an "Oohh MY GOD!!!" I didn't think the heavens could help me.

He kneeled down, pulling me toward the end of the bed and his mouth touched me and wreaked havoc on my opening. As his tongue twirled and leaped around my clit. I clenched the sheets as the sexual tension built. I came so hard it devoured his entire mouth. He sat there dripping, leaking of my love lemonade.

Jay

"You taste so good." I let her know as I wiped my face with a nearby towel. Letting her know that it was no big deal and that I enjoyed every moment of it.

Propping herself from the bed, gasping for air, she was spent. She collected herself. She stood, dropping the sheet to the floor. Revealing her and all of her glory. She was beautiful, goddess like even. Sex drunk, she approached me. She licked her lips, with a menacing look on her face. It was as if the pleasure I gave her was seen as a challenge, and she would not admit defeat tonight.

She removed my shirt, draping it to the floor. Pressing her body against my hardness. She kneeled down to and slipped off my pants and boxers with one fell swoop, and revealed the treasure she'd been yearning for from the start.

As her fingers ran up and down my shaft, I eased back onto the bed, slightly tilting my head back. She then wrapped her hands around my girth and stroked gently. I could feel myself growing harder with each stroke. She then slipped my dick into her mouth. I gasped and clenched the sheets as she caught me off guard.

Damn, if her mouth felt this good, I could only imagine what her pussy felt like.

"Shit." The word escaped my lips as her tongue twirled across the tip. I felt myself on the verge of cumming so I pulled her up. It was too soon, and I had to make sure I handled my business, play time was over.

I brought her up to me, facing me, I cradled her breasts, taking them into my mouth and sucking. Her head flung back in innate pleasure as she straddled me. Grabbing her ass, I eased her onto me and slowly inched inside of her. Damn, she was so tight. Traci claimed me as she bucked, popped, twerked, and grinded on my dick. I stood up to lay her on the bed, and she wrapped her legs around my waist. So, I did what any respectable man would do, I fed it to her standing up. We moved as one; it was beyond intense. I felt my legs grow weak. She felt so good. I turned and laid her on the high pillow top mattress, plunging into her as she bit her lip and screamed, "Oh, shit!"

That just made me want to go in even deeper, plunging until I hit the brick wall at the back of her uterus. I continued in a quick, powerful pace as I could tell that we were about to both climaxed. I reached her spot, and it too screamed out like a trapped love goddess. The pleasure grew as she tightened her walls around me. Letting out a deep breath, I tried to regain my composure.

It started with her feet. She shook, braced and clenched on to whatever she could get a hold of. She came; her body stiffened, eyes tightened and then fell limp, basking in the sense of sexual relief. Only a moment later, with one last powerful thrust, I had succumbed to the same fate.I exploded and filled the condom with my satisfied swimmers.

Shit. She just had to be mine.

Traci

I laid naked on his chest, content and satisfied; the most I had ever been in my life. This experience was different. It was as if Jay was the conductor of his own musical and I was the soloist. He damn sure knew what he was doing, and he did it oh so well.

If there were more men like this out there in the world, then I had been missing out. Trevor wasn't the best in the bedroom, but I got past that because I loved him on a different level. It was more than just sex with him. Now that it is over, I am open to more options. I know that next time, if I were to be in another relationship, sexual satisfaction and fulfillment would be more of a priority. But I knew that I wasn't interested in being in a relationship anytime soon.

The cool breeze of the ceiling fan wisted across us as we laid sex funky in bed. We repositioned ourselves, catching our breath. It was damn sure worth every minute.

Three

Chapter 3

Traci

Nat and I were the proud owners of a personal concierge business based out of Los Angeles, California. Today was the day, the day that would make or break our company.

We had the meeting planned for months and it was finally here. We had been in business for a little over six years. Well in business for the last six years, but the last two years, the business had been booming. We had put in a lot of work. Over the last couple of months, we had gained several celebrity clients, athletes and high-profile professionals. Mr. Banks, a client we had been going back and forth with, was his assistant, and was the newest to add to our roster. For months we had been trying to make sure we met every one of his expectations. We left no stone unturned ensuring we dot our I's and crossed our T's. Dotting our I's and crossing our T's.

Mr. Banks was the one to know in Los Angeles. In as little as

Chapter 3

six months, Banks had transformed his idea into a multi-million dollar business. So, he was definitely the right one to grease our palms with! The entire time we were planning meetings and conducting business over the phone with his assistant. It felt weird that we were making important decisions and hadn't met him in person, but such as life. The money was right and he paid the bills in the end, so I let the thought leave as quickly as it came.

To my understanding, there would be five people at this meeting; Nat, myself, Mr. Banks, his assistant and one of his business partners, Mr. Stone. It would be interesting to finally meet the man that shelled out so much money in person.

Nat had arrived earlier that day to help set everything for the meeting. We prepped the table in the conference room with brochures of the property, refreshments, and contracts. We crossed our fingers, hoping the set-up was exquisite enough to impress.

The contract alone would bring our company a thousand dollar finder's fee, a twenty percent commission on all quarterly profits, an exclusive contract for expansion, and other services. An added bonus would be them passing the word on to other business associates and friends. So, this was a huge deal that we could not afford to mess up. And neither one of us attended too.

***

"So tell me about his man that had you all open." Nat insisted, wanting and waiting for all the details of my steamy love session.

"Oh, Girl!" Looking around to make sure no one was around to overhear the details of my thotty behavior. "It was soo good. Far better than anything I'd ever experienced with the one whose name shall remain nameless for the rest of this conversation. He licked, sucked, touched and pleased every part of me. Made me feel things in places that, —mmm." I could barely finish my thought before it sent a shiver down my spine.

"Girl, so what now? Are you going to see him again or what?"

"Nat, are you crazy? Did you forget that I just got out of a seven-year relationship? A relationship that I've been in since college. With a man who cheated on me with my own damn assistant!"

"Girl, you can't still be recovering from that. You knew he was no good when you met him. So him cheating on you shouldn't have come as a shock. Plus, he was wack; as a person and sexually. Move the fuck on!"

"Everybody can't be emotionally detached like you. But no, I'm going to take this time and focus. Just as I should have before Trevor. I invested too much of myself into him, when I should have invested more of my time into our business. We could have been further along, but you live and you learn. It won't happen again. No more interruptions from this thing called love. Plus, he lives in New York and I live in L.A. what's the chance of me seeing him again?"

***

11:45 am

Lisa greeted everyone as she walked into the conference room to advise us that Mr. Banks and Mr. Stone would be joining us shortly. She looked over the setup and appeared to be impressed. Things were starting off well already. During our conversations, I took a ton of notes. Taking everything into account. That

Chapter 3

was my expertise, Nat's were the numbers and meetings. I was more of the behind-the-scenes kind of girl.

After a moment of taking in the ambiance we created, Lisa received a call. She nodded in our direction to alert us that both men were here and the meeting could begin shortly. A sudden sense of nervousness came over me, and my palms began to sweat.

"Pull yourself together, Traci! You got this! This is what you worked for." I thought to myself, trying to calm my nerves, and letting out a sigh.

"Girl, we got this!" Nat confirmed, sensing my nervousness.

"Here they come." Nat said, tapping me on the shoulder. Alerting me of their arrival as I gathered my things to place them back in my bag.

In a bent down position, Lisa entered the room and as she did, addressed the gentleman as they proceeded after her. "Ladies, I'd like to introduce you to Mr. Kenneth Stone and Mr. Joseph Banks."

My mother-fucking, *excuse my language*, jaw dropped. I promise it was as if I was a deer caught in headlights.

Standing there before me was Mr. Rub Me all the right ways, Mr. Lickity Clit, Mr. Doran the Explorer himself; Joseph "Jay" Banks. The owner of Simple Touch, my client and the whole reason for this meeting.

What THE Entire FUCK?!

Father God, if you could hear my internal cry. Please let me remain calm during this ordeal. Let this meeting go smoothly and according to plan. Father. I ask you now to forgive me. Lord, I may have done some UNGODLY things the days prior, but it was the man you sent me, Lord God. Getting off track,... Please Father, hear my humble cry. In your Heavenly Name, Amen.

I collected my thoughts and my emotions. "Nice to meet you both," I responded as professionally as I could. Without hesitation, I reached out to shake both of their hands and carried on the meeting all while trying to pretend nothing had happened between me and Jay. But in my mind I thought, did he know and was toying with me the whole time? Was he just as shocked as I was?

He sat across from me, and he seemed so cavalier. Was this a normal occurrence for him? To sleep with the help and watch them squirm doing a meeting, to see if they can keep their composure? My mind ran in circles. I felt like Jimmy Neutron when he came up with his contraptions and calculations. Enter input, probabilities and outputs. He had the right one today, though. I was going to handle this so cool, calm and collected; he wasn't gonna know what to do with himself. I refused to be played for a fool, by a man, again. I promise I'm done with men and their whole species. I guess now this is a great time to see what I can get into on the other side of the fence.

I collected my thoughts as I continued with my introduction. I could automatically feel his eyes on me. Flashbacks of our moment together suddenly rushed to memory. I quickly quieted my thoughts, tried to avoid eye contact and proceeded with the presentation.

"So gentlemen, the brochure before you is of the entire property with highlighted amenities, accessible to you and your clients. There is also the contract with the terms as we discussed in our prior conversations. A spreadsheet with the agreed upon financial information has already been calculated. We have also included a list of services provided by our company that we think may be beneficial to you. Those services have the potential to contribute to your growth and ideals for further

Chapter 3

expansion. Marketing material and contact information have been included in your folders. So fellas, taking all the line items that you required as well as some that you thought could add to your business into consideration, I believe we have gone above and beyond your expectations. With that being said, I think that Already Booked would be a perfect fit for your brand. What do you say?"

Feeling confident with the presentation I let out another deep sigh. It was finally over. All the prep work, planning, going back and forth and stress was over. But even after all that, there was still a lingering problem at hand. If they go forward with the proposal, where will that leave *us*?

Jay
a few hours before the meeting

I spent the rest of my time thinking about Traci and our night together. We held each other. She shared all of her past hurt with me. I was the shoulder she needed, which I had no problem lending. The next morning she left without notice, I guess she shared too much and that embarrassed her. Like they always say: if it's meant to be, then it will be.

I have been in other relationships before. Nothing ever too serious. Ending always on a mutual note. No one ever cheated; it just seemed to fizzle out. I had always been attracted to ambitious women. Having the same principles and values, it was no surprise that business always came before a relationship, but at this point in my life, I was ready to settle down. My business was successful; it could run on its own. It was the perfect time to focus on me. At twenty-nine, it was time to focus on the finer things in life. Getting married, having a family, the whole nine. After just one encounter, I was willing to risk it all for her … for Traci.

Get it together, Jay!

She had made her choice, and she chose to leave, so it was time for me to focus on the business. Everything else would have to wait.

I ran the water of the shower to freshen up for the day. The meeting wasn't until noon. I had time; it was only nine. I laid my tailored, pressed suit, white button up, with plain gold cufflinks, and a pair of shiny black closed lace oxfords across the bed.

As the water dripped from my back, from the shower head. It felt like fingertips. My thoughts threaded back to her. Her mouth on mine, how she felt, her touch. Why couldn't I shake the thought of her? What made her so special, so unique? Shit. I had to find her. After, everything is said and done. Jumping out of the shower, the phone rang. It was Lisa, letting me know she will be waiting in the lobby with Mr. Stone for our meeting. I notified her I will be down in 15.

I got dressed, took a shot of Henny to clear my head and made my way to the lobby.

*****

It was a quarter till noon; I am always sure to arrive at all my meetings and business arrangements at least thirty minutes early. Lisa briefed me on everything that I needed to be filled in on and so did Mr. Stone. Everything looked good on our end, so the decision was already set. Going through the entire presentation just made things look more official and less rushed. I guess it was like making them sweat, to see if they can handle the pressure. To get a feel for who I'm doing business with and what areas I can take them to in further business ventures. I did the same with Lisa and Mr. Stone. It builds strength and shows character.

Chapter 3

While receiving my briefing; as we inched toward the conference room, there she was. The woman who had my thoughts captive since that night in the bar. The woman we had been in contact with this entire time was *her*. Traci Carter. Fate, My Funny Twisted Companion. You sure got me this time. I was glad I noticed when I did. I could only imagine the shock she would endure when she saw that it was me. I had to tell her, and hopefully she will be just as surprised as I am about the situation. e

"Sir, I have some paperwork here I need you to sign before we go into the meeting." Lisa said, handing me a stack of papers.

Fuck.

"Can't it wait?" I tried to rush by her to exit the room. "I'm afraid not, sir. It's regarding the finalizations for the location in L.A. They need your attention as soon as possible so they can continue with the project."

"Well enough, let me have it," I replied, taking the paperwork from her. There was no time. I guess we would just have to see how everything played out.

* * *

Traci was a true professional. She handled the situation well. No one ever would have guessed that we were bumping uglies forty-eight hours ago. She played it off well, because I know it wasn't forgettable; not with all of the shits, damns, and name calling she was doing. Her level of professionalism was impressive. Even still, I had to advise her that I had no idea.

Traci

Papers were signed and the meeting was done. So glad this

shit was over with. It took everything inside me not to lash out and give this man a piece of my mind. That's what I get again for trusting a man, again. Well, I guess I can't completely blame him. I was there. Just as he was. One-night stands hardly ever play out well. This was just one of those times. Just when I felt that I could be vulnerable again, it was just another slap from love. I truly didn't know if he knew, all I knew was that it could never happen again.

"You mean to tell me, you… and him…" Nat said in shock after I let her know of the foolishness I got myself into. "Ooh girl, the scandal! But you know all I wanna know is, you gonna do it again?" Unable to continue being embarrassed, I had to give it to my best friend, the real. "Girl, it was *the* BEST I have ever had. My body sang in octaves I didn't know were possible, it was amazing." "So, bitch. What are you going to do now? I mean with him being our new boss/partner and all." "What do you mean, what am I going to do? It's over. That was the first and the last time. You know things never go well when you mix business with pleasure."

"Girl shit, you just told me you had some mind blowing sex. This guy has his *own* money, is rich, a nice guy and fine as fuck and you ain't gonna see what's up with that?"

"That's right! I can't. I can't chance something going wrong with a "relationship" if it jeopardizes our business. The business that we worked so hard to get to where we are now. I will not. The last time I put some 'guy' before work it put our business on the back burner. I will not do that again. I refuse." "Trac, I promise I understand. But guys like this come a dime a dozen. I don't want you to miss out on something that could be good, maybe even great for you. Just be sure you take all things into consideration before shunning it all off. You know I love you

Chapter 3

girl and only want the best for you. But don't just continue thru life mad at the world because of one stupid idiot. He wasn't worth anything to begin with. To me, finding out he wasn't shit was the best thing that could have happened to you. At least you didn't end up marrying that fool, we would have been talking about divorce instead of a failed relationship.

She was right. Man, did I wish she wasn't? Nat always had been the voice of reason, and I hated it. Why couldn't she just have seen things my way? But that's what it means to have a genuine friend. We love each other good, bad or indifferent. We always gave each other the advice we needed to hear and not just what one wanted.

Chapter 4

Traci

After celebrating and telling my shame to Nat at the bar, it was time to call it a night. The day had brought enough stress and I just needed a reset. Plus, the alcohol was settling. So, before I could spend any more time in Jamaica making poor decisions, I needed to go to my room and lock myself in solitude.

"Well girl, you ain't gonna put an end to my fun. I'm going to see if this Stella can get her groove back," Nat said matter-of-factly.

"Well you have fun with that. Please let me know when you get in so I know that you're safe. I'll see you in the morning."

"Ok, Mama!" she replied jokingly.

We said our goodbyes and I made my way back to my room. I had to pee like a racehorse, luckily there was a restroom downstairs in the lobby to use. "Woo, I made it. I said to myself as I released 1/10th of the alcohol I had consumed just moments

Chapter 4

before. No more rum punch for me, water for the rest of the trip. Glad I'm leaving tomorrow. I exited the bathroom to continue my journey to my room, when I came across the hotel announcement. Coming Soon! Simple Touch Massage Clinical Services, with a picture of Mr. Simple Touch himself. Damn, I couldn't seem to escape this guy for one day. Not only did he haunt my thoughts, but I also had to get a visual reminder as well. The reminder of how fine he was.

Snap out of it, girl. You have to get him out of your head.

I took my time as I stumbled to the elevator and down the hall to my room. Trying to focus, I concentrated as I read the numbers on the doors of the rooms. I hurried to put the key in the right door, trying not to disturb any one with my mess.

Room 414, finally. I anxiously opened the door and staggered in. Glad to be in my room, off my feet and away from everything. I turned on the T.V. as I undressed to get ready to take a shower. An infomercial of island living came on and I just left it there, it wasn't like there was anything else on this time of night, anyway. I didn't pay much attention to it, anyway. Soon enough, the sandman carried me off to sleep. Well, it was either him or the liquor.

I pinned up my locs and got in the shower. The water was so refreshing. Nothing like a shower after a long day. Especially the long day that I had. I draped myself in a white robe and laid in the bed. It didn't make much sense to get completely dressed when it was so hot, plus I was drunk and alone. Who was I covering up for? As I laid there, I turned the tv off and put on some music instead. Trey Songz rang out, reminding me of how he invented sex.

Great, exactly what I needed. To be reminded of sex.

Since Trey has sparked up a desire in me, it didn't make sense to let a good feeling go to waste.

The song took me back … it led me right back to good memorable sex. It was at this moment I was glad I always made sure to pack my trusty little love bunny. The *bunny* also kept me faithful anytime I traveled when I was in a relationship.

"You would never cheat on me or do me dirty, would you? You always come through when I need you most," I said looking at my twelve speed rabbit vibe I pulled out of my bag. We had become even further acquainted since the breakup.

I set the scene as if I was really about to indulge in a true sexual encounter; laughing at myself when I thought about how pitiful this was. *It is what it is.*

I lit my favorite candle. Yes, I traveled with my candles. They bring calm in stressful situations. Plus, there was something about smelling the sweet aroma and listening to Trey Songz while pleasuring yourself.

Zzzzzzzz… The bunny hummed.

And the games began; my body shuttered. Dive in nnn….mmm mm. I bit the corner of my lip, as one hand penetrated my lower regions and the other caressed my breast. Yessss. I threw my hips, thrusting as if there were actually someone there to receive the love I was giving. "Ohhhh shit." Within minutes I climaxed.

Visions of Jay danced in my head, I shuttered again. God, if only he was here. Talking to me sexually, touching me, giving me what I'd missed for all those years — giving me what I'd missed since the last time he touched me. Mmmm, just the thought of him made me orgasm again.

As my juices flowed onto the now dampened sheets, I heard a knock at the door. It had to be Nat; she was the only one that knew the room I was in. Plus, she must be letting me know that

Chapter 4

she was turning in for the night.

I opened the drawer to put my friend up, slipped my panties and robe back on. "Nat, you know you could have just called—" I called out, but was shocked to see that my words were directed to the wrong person. "Jay, or should I say Joseph… What are you doing here?"

Entering the room and offering no response, he lifted me up by my waist. Placing me in a straddling position. Remaining silent, he carried me and placed me upon the dresser. Without wasting any time he pulled my panties down.

He kissed my inner thigh as he played with my clit with his fingers. My head immediately fell back in immense pleasure. In his deep baritone voice, he chimed, "You wet for me already, baby?" He was so confident, not knowing that I had just satisfied myself just moments prior.

Instead of busting his bubble, I let him continue and think that was the case, because he wasn't wrong. Jay had been the inspiration for the scene I'd just played out. "Mmmm," I moaned.

Taking his tongue as he ran laps around my opening, continuing to stroke me with his fingers. He knew exactly what to do and how to get me there. Already puddling over his tongue, he continued to work his magic as my legs twitched. I felt an electric sensation surge through my body and I shuttered again.

As he came up from my love box; mouth smothered in my love, he kissed me passionately. I didn't mind tasting myself, and at the moment I really didn't even care. He felt beyond good, and hell it's mine. I'm a freak anyway, so shit like that didn't even bother me. He stepped back to remove my robe and bra; releasing my voluptuous size D breasts. He gathered them in his hands as if they were his last meal and took them into his mouth.

"Oh my God." The swelling between my legs was uncontrollable. I wanted him— I wanted him right then!!

Jay

I picked her up from the dresser and carried her to the bed. Before I could get her there, she had grabbed my piece. She stroked and placed it inside of her. Her love felt like a vice as she contracted herself around my dick. Traci rocked her hips in a circular motion as I gripped her ass.

Shit, she felt so good.

Kissing her deeply, I placed her against the wall. Sliding in and out of her. Her motions met mine, as we moved in unison. My body grew weak as I felt my legs buckle. I took her from the wall to the bed as we continued our love exodus. My strokes became more animalistic, more intense as I felt my climax approaching. I knew she did too as she dug her fingertips into my back.

"Yes, baby. Oh Shit!" She screamed as I dove deeper. She removed her hand from my back to grip the sheets. I threw her legs onto my shoulders. I made every attempt to touch her thoughts with my stick, engraving the memory of us on her mind. Each gesture, each kiss and touch was an apology. I needed her to know that I was sorry for the prior day's events.

With every thrust, I felt like my body was about to explode.

"Shhh Ittt, I'm about to cum," I growled.

I grabbed her ankles as I dug in deeper moments before my climax. I backed up, coming halfway out, leaving the tip in and pushing it back in again. Leaving her spent, I released her legs allowing them to slide down beside us. My hands explored her body passing over the hardened peaks of her breasts, then landed on her shoulders— her shoulders that I grabbed and

Chapter 4

used as leverage to ramp up my thrusts. The motions were in triple time until I reached an explosion and our bodies fell limp. Filling her with all of me. Hopefully that would be just the ticket for her to forgive me so we could get past everything and move forward.

"We can not do this again," she said, as she caught her breath.

Searching her eyes for reasoning. "How can you deny yourself from something that feels so good?" I questioned.

"Look, I've done this whole song and dance before, and I refuse to go through it again. I know that you are and seem to be a really nice man, but I just can't. Wounds are still fresh and I need time."

"Traci, some time? Really? That man didn't love you, couldn't have cared less about you. Why would you dismiss the feelings we have for each other? It's almost as if we are kindred spirits, we just gravitated to each other. How else can you explain all of this?"

"Coincidence. Let me ask you a question. Did you know? Did you who I was before the first time we had sex?"

"Of course, not! What kind of person do you think I am?"

"Exactly, Sir! I don't know you and you don't know me."

"But I want to get to know you. I want you to know me and I want to get to know you as well." "And you will, just not on this level. Had we met on different terms, maybe it would have been different? But right now, Mr. Banks, it's been nice but I think you should leave." She dismissed me.

"Traci, you can't be serious."

She stood up, placed on her robe, and walked to the door. "I'm sorry, but this has to end."

Giving her a disconcerted look, I respected her wishes, and I left.

Traci

My eyelids slammed shut and I sighed heavily. It didn't take me long to regret my decision after I closed the door.

But I had to—right?

I have been working toward this for so long. Love and relationships could not be the reason I had another setback. At twenty-eight I didn't have anything, but this business. In my mind a college graduate my age should have been more established than I was. Too much of my time was spent on a man. A man that had it all, while I had nothing. This time I was choosing me. Gone were the days where I put everyone ahead of myself. That ship had sailed, and everything else besides my business had to take a back seat in my life. Not be the reason behind another set back. I am 28 and have nothing to show for it all but this business. For a college graduate, I have to be more established than this. I spent too much time behind a man; he had it all, and I had nothing. So that ends now. Everything else will have to take a back seat!

Chapter 5

Traci

Back to reality, I tried so desperately to escape. Returning at least on a better note. I had more contracts to write, clients to contact, and a cheating ass ex to dodge.

Unfortunately, we still lived together. My stuff was still there. Six months ago when I caught him nestled between that bitch's legs. I was on the first thing smoking. I hopped in my car and headed straight to the only place that I could find peace, Nat's House. I knew my girl would welcome me with open arms. With my mom being in Dallas and my Aunt and Uncle far too far to drive, Nat had always been the closest thing to a family I had.

I figured it was that, or end up another episode on the First 48.

I planned the mission perfectly. At 10:15, I landed and by 11:25; I made it home. Well, to that house I used to call home.

Love Interrupted

I knew that Trevor would be at work. So there would be no chance of running into him. I asked Nat to meet me over here so we could grab all my things at one time. So after today, I would not have any worries about coming back.

I walked into the house, I checked my messages. I left my personal phone at Nat's, so I would have the peace of mind that was necessary. Plus, I wouldn't have to deal with the likes of Trevor.

The message played and it was Trevor.

"Baby, I'm sorry. Please let me explain. Call me to let me know that you're alright. I love you."

Explain what, how she tricked you and landed on ya dick and ya'll just started fucking? You Love me? Nigga, please!

"Babe, please pick up. We need to talk. Call Me!"

Yeah, we need to talk alright! Talk about how you's a worthless ass nigga. And how I'm mad as fuck I wasted six years of my life, when I could have been with that big dick nigga in Jamaica, or at least somebody like it.

"Traci, you need to call me. Let's be adults about this!"

Adults??!!?? What's so being adults about fucking my assistant, nigga? I pay her! Hope her pussy was sunshine, cause you never get this again.

Let's be adults about this? How would you expect a girl to react after the man you were supposed to spend your life with gets caught ass up, balls deep in some random bitch? Late at work, my ass.

I should have known that things were different. My business was booming; I spent more time traveling and making plans for clients than spending time with him. I have to admit, how things turned out was partly my fault. But that would have been grounds for a conversation or taking action like counseling, but definitely not cheating. It was no secret that I worked from

Chapter 5

home and spent late nights on the computer; admittedly letting the sun catch me still hard at it the next morning. I was a night owl, so I was at my best during the wee hours.

After listening to the messages, I snapped out of it and realized, there wouldn't be anymore waking up next to Trevor in the morning. He was gone and it was over. Gone were the days of receiving flowers, and Trevor serving me breakfast in bed. Everything that was *us*, no longer existed … including our non-existing sex life.

We gathered the rest of my belongings and packed them into the back of Nat and my trucks. Luckily, everything that I had and wanted to take fit perfectly between the two of us. We were done with enough time to spare. The trip was a success. Avoid the Ex at all cost! Mission Complete!

* * *

When we made it to Nat's house I was able to get settled down, for the first time in awhile. My life had been a whirlwind. Up and down emotions, not knowing what to do from one point to the next. I was glad to breathe a sigh of relief. But I guess the relief would have to wait.

My peace was interrupted by a ringing, a ringing that came from the phone in my purse. I don't know what I was thinking or why would I even bother… it was my mother. I could have waited till tomorrow for this call. Maybe it was better this way. I didn't need this depressing conversation to carry me into a new day.

"Hey Mom."

"Hey Baby, how you doing?"

"I'm good, how about yourself?"

"I'm good, just checking on you, baby. Making sure you're ok."

Here it comes.

"You know, I just got off the phone with Trevor. He told me you moved all your stuff outta the house."

"Yeah, mom. I told you, he and I are no longer together."

"Baby, why not? You too made the cutest couple. You were on the path to marriage and everything."

"I told you mama, I can't be with someone I can't trust. I want to be in a relationship that makes me happy. And definitely not one of convenience."

"But he has that good job at IBM. I know he's gonna take care of you."

"But mama, you remember he cheated. God knows how many times. I can't be with someone that doesn't respect me enough to stay committed. What would be the whole point of that? Stay in a relationship, knowing that there is a possibility that he might do it again."

"Trac, he's a man. They are gonna do what they are gonna do. Maybe if you would focus more time on him than on that little business of yours it wouldn't make it so easy for him to wonder."

"*Really* mama?"

"I'm just saying, men need attention. And if you weren't so busy, he wouldn't have had to go seek it from somebody else."

"Ok, mama. What about the fact that he can't keep his hands to himself?"

"Trac, that was one time. He already said he wasn't himself that day and it would never happen again." He said he wouldn't do it again."

"One time thing? He wasn't himself? He shouldn't have done

Chapter 5

it in the first place. I could already see that this conversation was going nowhere. Just like all the conversations before, when the whole "Trevor" subject came up...

"Mama, I love you. But I'm not about to do this right now. I'm exhausted. I just want to relax. I'll call you tomorrow. Love you, mama.

"Ok, baby. I love you too. You know—"

I hung up.

I couldn't take anymore of that conversation. I knew my mom just wanted the best for me, but clearly didn't see Trevor was not it. I didn't know what I could do to make her see, so she wouldn't bring him up anymore. Trevor was quite a charmer; hell he charmed the hell out of me. That charming quality he possessed is what ended our relationship. Something about him charming the next bitch out of her panties didn't sit well with me.

I laid in bed and reminisced. The conversation I had with my mom took me back to my relationship with Trevor. my thoughts with memories of my relationship with Trevor.. My thoughts were flooded with memories. All of them— both good and bad, but mainly the bad ones...Staring up at the bright, white ceiling was like looking at a blank canvas. The room made me drift back to a night — the night everything ended between me and Trevor.

"If only you could have been there, babe. It was crazy! The cashier was so rude. I almost slapped the dog shit outta her." I called out to Trevor as I placed our takeout on the kitchen counter. He didn't answer back. I knew he was at home, his car was parked outside. *Surely*, he couldn't have fallen asleep this early. I placed my bag on the chair, grabbed a glass of wine to ease the tension and I started back to the bedroom. It seemed unusually dark, but I dismissed the thought. The lights being off could have easily been explained, like maybe he was in the shower or lying down. I checked to see if he was in the bedroom; he wasn't there either.

Where was he?

I removed my shoes to get comfortable, and placed them in the closet. t I decided to get some water ready for a bath. Trevor would show up eventually. I was too tired to play hide and seek, but maybe he was in the den. He often spent time there when he had a difficult time going to sleep. I placed my glass on the oversized porcelain tub, as I ran the water, sprinkling my Lavender scented Epsom salt and bubble bath. I placed my hand in the stream to mix the soothing additives together in the water. This combination always made my body feel great after a long day. As I wrapped my hair and put on my bonnet, I heard a noise coming from the office — my office.

What the hell was he doing in there?

I walked down the hallway from my room, Miguel's "How Many Drinks," was playing in the background. I loved that song! I began unbuttoning my top. That song always got me in the mood. I moved to open the door and I couldn't believe my eyes. My heart dropped. There was my man, hitting some bitch from the back. Spread eagle on **my** *motherfucking* desk. A desk **I** paid for; to conduct **MY** business.

This disrespectful motherfucker!

It was at that moment; my soul left my body…..

Chapter 6

Traci

This motherfucker done lost his fucking mind.

Cheating on me, in the house we lived in together, with this fucking bitch; my fucking assistant.

I couldn't believe this worthless bastard. Everybody tried to warn me about Trevor, but I was too blinded by love to listen. I couldn't believe that I was so wrapped up in his lies that I stayed and wasted seven fucking years of my life.

Catching him in that moment made me feel as if my body had levitated to get a better view of what would transpire next. I wasn't myself. Anger rushed over me and while my assistant was riding my man into tomorrow, I yanked her ass up. She landed on the other side of my desk and cowered into the corner in fear. I continued on and wasted seven fucking years of my life.

At that moment it seemed as if I was levitating over my body, as I watched what happened next. It didn't even seem like I was myself. Anger rushed over me. As she so gallantly rode my man into no tomorrow, I yanked that bitch up. She fell off to the other side of the bed and cowered in the corner in fear.

I jumped on him so quickly, giving him a good ole L.A. ass whooping that he was oh so deserving of. I completely lost it. The days of being simple and fucking up the bitch were long gone, even though in this situation she should have known better. This ass whooping today was all his, because he acted on his temptation. "How the fuck could you! With this bitch!" I yelled as I pointed to Toren still in the same spot from where I tossed her ass.

All I could hear from her was that she was sorry. She kept saying it, repeatedly.

"I don't want ya sorries bitch. Just get your shit and get the fuck up outta my house before I forget myself and you get a dose of what I just gave to him. Toren gathered her clothes and made a beeline for the door.

"Consider me not whooping your severance pay, Bitch; 'cause you're fired! I don't want to see your face around here ever again. And for your sake, I hope you had a contingency plan, because this Nigga doesn't have shit! Hope it was worth it." I yelled out to her before she closed the door.

"And you," I directed at Trevor. "You no good, motherfucker! How could you? I gave you everything. I … I left my family … everything I've ever known for your bitch ass. Then you turn around and treat me like shit for some side pussy. I hope it was worth losing everything because we're done!"

"No baby, it wasn't even like that" he cried, trying to find an explanation.

"I bet you were probably cheating on me this entire time. You

Chapter 6

make me sick. You know what you can have all of this shit. I don't even want it! I'm glad my girl convinced me to keep my own shit."

"But baby, let me explain," he pleaded, reaching for me to keep me from leaving.

"Don't you fucking touch me!"

The audacity of this dude!

To try to touch me with the same hands he just got finished touching that bitch with.

Lost your damn mind.

I packed as many clothes as I could in my suitcase and made my way to my car. I knew I probably shouldn't drive in my condition, but I had to get out of there, and quickly before I did something that I would regret and would get to set up residency in the County Jail. but I had to get out of there and get out of there quickly. Before I did something that I would regret and end up as a resident at the County Jail. I worked too hard to get to where I was, and I would not let this bastard jeopardize everything I built.

Reaching for the door, I felt a sting shoot up my arm and radiate to my shoulder. I turned, and I realized Trevor had grabbed me.

Wow, I guess tonight was full of first times.

"Have you lost your damn mind, grabbing me like that?"

"Look calm, down. It wasn't what you think."

The infamous line.

"Look, I'm not even going to play into your bullshit right now. Let my arm go before this whole thing gets blown way too far out of proportion. You are hereby free to do whatever and with whoever you want. I'm not about to argue or make a scene."

"I'm not letting you go until you come here and we talk this thing out," he said persistently.

"There's nothing else for us to talk about. We're done, so just let me go."

"We're not going to be done until I say we're done."

Yet another first.

Did this nigga think I was a hostage? What kind of shit is that, I can' leave until he says? I was so confused. Maybe the last six years was a complete lie because he had no clue who I was. Tonight was the perfect night to give him a reminder.

"I'm telling you this one last time, let go of my *fucking* arm so I can leave, *or* there's going to be a problem. "

"You not going nowhere until I'm fi—"

And before he could finish his sentence, the lamp on the nightstand met the back of his head. He stumbled back, trying to regain his composure. When he did, he reached up and grabbed a hold of me yet again.

"Are you fucking crazy, have you lost your mind?" He asked with disbelief in his voice.

"I don't know, have you?" I responded as I kneed him in the groin. Down went Frazier.

"I could care less about the pain you're feeling now. We could have avoided all of this. If you were only upfront in the first damn place. Not lookatcha! Please remember, I am not one of your little girlfriends. The next time you put

your hands on me, and hopefully for your sake there won't be a next time. I'ma kill you!" Not waiting for a response, I left. At that point, I hope I'd never see his face again.

Racing down the 405 like a bat out of hell, looking every which way paranoid. Not trying to get pulled over while in distress. I called my girl before I reached her house, to let her know that I was on my way.

Chapter 6

"Hey Trac! What's up, girl?" she sounded half asleep.

"Nat, I'm on the way to your house. I need a place to stay for a bit."

"Girl, what happened? Is everything ok? What's wrong?" she said drilling me with one hundred and one questions.

"I'll tell you when I get there. Can't really talk too much over the phone right now. I'll be there in a few." I said hanging up.

I pulled up to her house. It was damn near midnight. I didn't know that it was actually that late. No wonder she sounded asleep, it was late. With all that was going on I didn't even realize. Good thing we owned our own business. At a time like this, getting ready for the biggest meeting of my career and this...I can't.

"That sorry son of a bitch did what? With who? Toren?"

I sat and ran the whole story down to her. Scene by scene. "I was surprised that you didn't kill that motherfucker."

"I was so close girl! Oh so close. It was almost as if I blacked out."

"Shid, I would have too. Blacked out and black the som' bitches eye! For real, you handled that situation well ... or at least better than I would have. Kudos to you girl. You can definitely stay here as long as you want to. Onto a lighter note, not to make it seem like your problems aren't worth a discussion. But are you ready to go to Jamaica? Ready to turn all the way up. No strings." Nat asked.

"I'm ready for this trip to get the contact, but as far as the turn up is concerned. I don't know about that yet. It's still too much, too soon." Massaging my temples. "I'm tired, girl. Can we just talk about all this tomorrow?

"That's right girl! We have a lot of prepping to do before the trip, so need you well rested. Get some rest."

I just wanted to close my eyes, and dream that all of this was just a nightmare. Even if the thought was highly unlikely.

It was around nine in the morning when I woke up. I felt like I had been hit by a ton of bricks. Just drained emotionally, exhausted. Traci, you have to snap out of this. You have a business to run and you have work to do. Trying to muster any kind of motivation, to get myself through the day.

You can do this girl!

I went out to my car and grabbed my bags to settle in. Came back in to look inside Nat's fridge to see what she had to cook up. Eggs, Milk, Cheese, Water. Damn she must never eat at home. Forget this I'll just order something from GrubHub.

Well I waited for my food, I checked my email and voicemails. A bunch of calls from potential clients, trying to get rates on certain trips, Mr. Banks' assistant calling of meeting and trip confirmation, and a bunch of calls from Trevor.

Hello, my name is Stephanie and I was referred to you by Tanya. I am planning a corporate trip for August and I wanted to get the best rates possible. Tanya said that you could help me with this. If you could please give me a call, (555) 682-4535. Thank you and look forward to hearing from you soon. Beep. Message Saved

Hey Traci, this is Lisa. Just calling to the confirmation the dates and time for the trip to Jamaica. If you could, please give me a call back at your earliest convenience. Talk to you soon.

Beep. Message Deleted

Baby, please give me a call back. We can get through this. Come back home so we can talk. Beep. Message Deleted

Hey baby, I know you got my message. Call me back.

Beep. Message Deleted

Traci, stop acting like a child! Call me back!

Beep. Message Deleted

Chapter 6

A child, this son of a bitch had the audacity to call me a child? But who's out there acting like a little boy that can't keep his dick in his pants. With a whole fiance! We were supposed to be getting married at the beginning of next year. The date was set, invitations had already been sent out. Like what the fuck! Our seventh anniversary was coming up! Seven years! Seven fucking years, wasted!!! For nothing! I can't believe it. He could have just told me he was no longer happy. I would have understood. I would have understood that over fucking my assistant! Almost made me wish that I had gotten married to his bitch ass. Just to make his life hell and take him for everything he's got! But hell, he wouldn't have even benefitted me any, that nigga doesn't even have shit anymore. I would have probably ended up owing!

"Morning Sis!"

"Morning, Girl."

"How d'you sleep?

"Bout as good as I could. What about yourself?"

"Good. Are you ready to get to work?"

"Definitely. I need something to keep my mind occupied."

"Well, Let's get to it."

I briefed her on the messages I received, and she did the same with the ones she had. We took down some notes, made a couple of calls and checked rates.

"Girl after this meeting with Mr. Banks, we're going to be on top of the world. I can already see this is going to open a lot of doors for us!"

"Yes! I can't wait! Things are going so well! Hard work really pays off."

"Sorry to bring it up while on such a pleasant note, but did you get a call from you know who?" "Yeah, I did."

"What did he say?" she said, trying to sound concerned.

"That he was sorry, you know the usual cheater b.s. I can't be consumed with all that right now, though. I need to take care of this and then worry about that later."

"I understand girl, so let's get this money!"

Seven

Chapter 7

Jay

"Damn, she treated you like one of the fellas. And it has you out here looking like a whole simp," Ant said with no care how what he said would affect my already depressed state.

"I thought she was feeling me. This one seemed different from the rest."

"She probably would have been different, if you two didn't have to work together." "But what difference does that make, really?"

"Please, you know that business and personal rarely ever work out. Someone eventually gets hurt, and that tarnishes the working relationship. All she's doing is preventing the inevitable." "How could she know, if we don't even try?"

"Again, like I said, what happens if you do and it doesn't? What would you lose?" I thought back on what Ant said. What would I lose, what would she lose? It was a decision that would

Love Interrupted

take some thought. I definitely needed to think this through with my big head and not my other one.

"Your right, Ant! She keeps insisting that we should keep it professional. So that's exactly what I'm going to do. Clear my thoughts of her and keep it strictly business. Thanks for the talk, bro." "Aye, you know I've had your back since grade school. Always have, always will. Ant had been my boy for as long as I could remember. We played ball in high school together. Even though we had gone to different colleges, we remained close. Growing up being the only child he was the closest and only thing that I had to a brother.

"Hey, with all that being said…she got a homegirl?"

"Oh, I can't be with her, but you're gonna try to get at her homegirl?"

"Hey, that's y'all business, but you could still hook a brother up!"

I scoffed, grabbing the basketball from his grasp. Continuing to play the game we started before we were distracted with conversation.

* * *

The next morning, I decided to see what L.A. had to offer. Being a New York native, getting accustomed to the west coast lifestyle, I knew it was going to be a change.

I figured I would take myself on a shopping trip. I would have to say that fashion wasn't one of my strong suits. A lot of my clothes scream that I wasn't from here. So if I decided that I was going to become a resident here, I will need to look that part.

It was a beautiful day in sunny California. 76 degrees, cool

Chapter 7

breeze; a brother could get used to this kind of weather. Back home, the weather would have never been like this. Had me thinking the song by Toni Tony Tone was the truth.

I took a stroll down to the Westfield Mall, noticing that it was in proximity to where I was staying. Figured I'd give it a shot.

I picked up some pairs of jeans, slack, t-shirt, dress shirts, and shoes. It was a pleasant experience. Glad I took the time to do so. Now I have everything that I need to make a great impression on the staff at tomorrow's meeting.

Valet parked the car at the tall towered building at exactly 11:30. As always, thirty minutes before a potential business meeting. I walked into the exquisitely decorated office building. Everything was neat and put into place. Plus the decor was phenomenal. Whoever decorated this place, I must have them when it came down to design my L.A. office.

I continued to walk the halls of the office. Everyone was busy at work when I laid my eyes on her. It had been over a month since the last time I saw her. Over a month since she shot me down. Don't get me wrong it was completely understandable, but it was not expected. I was used to women falling all over me and trying to be with me because I was well off and well known. I made New York's most eligible bachelors' list three years in a row. To everyone else they saw that as an accomplishment, to me I saw it as loneliness.

She sat with her head buried in her computer, in her glass paned office. Black blazer and slacks, black red bottoms and black-rimmed glasses to match. The outfit she wore looked like it did a magnificent job of accentuating all of my favored parts on her. And when she stood, it did just that. Instantly sending my thoughts back to me kissing, licking and sucking all of her, snatched back to the present by the calling of a familiar voice.

"Mr. Banks, the meeting is this way. Can I offer you any refreshments while you wait? My partner will be in to join us shortly." Nat said, pointing me and the direction of the meeting hall. Bringing to Traci's attention that I was standing in her presence. She hadn't noticed me there the entire time as I stood in admiration. I was glad that she didn't.

"No, thank you, Nat." breaking myself from the trance.

"You and Traci did a magnificent job on decorating the new office. Who did you get to do the decor?" "That was all Traci, she has a great eye for that kind of thing."

Really, I thought. Wondering, given our history, would she be up to doing the same for my office building? Wouldn't hurt to ask.

Through the glass paned double doors was a beautiful conference area. Adorn with black art, a custom wood table, with matching custom chairs.

"Traci, put her time into all of this didn't she," I said, taking my time to admire the furnishings. "Not really, she did everything fairly quickly. She just has a knack for this sort of thing." Just then, Traci walked into the room.

"Mr. Banks was just telling us how he admired the decor."

"Oh, really." She said, giving a look of appreciation. "It's nothing, really. I had the layout in my head and I figured I could save money just doing it myself."

"Resourceful."

"Well, I know you didn't come all this way just to talk about design and decor. How may we help you? Straight to the point, I like that. "Yes, the company has a retreat coming up and I need you to book the travel for 25 employees. This will include room, flight and transportation. Is this something that you could do?"

"Of course, we have no problem working that out for you.

Chapter 7

Will we have to contact Lisa for the details?"

"No, I would like to handle this all myself. Plus Traci, I have another proposition for you." "Of course, Nat and I can handle that as well."

"No this task is specially tailored for you."

"I'm just going to let you guys continue talking. It was nice talking to you, Mr. Banks." Nat said as she continued to walk out of the room.

"Nice talking to you also, Nat. Thanks again for everything."

Nat left the room, leaving us alone for the first time since Jamaica. Silence fell between us as I shifted in my chair to direct my attention toward her.

Breaking the silence, I cleared my thoughts. "Ms. Carter—"

"Traci." she interrupted.

"My apologies, Traci. After seeing what you have done with your office here. I would like to hire you to do my office buildings at our downtown location in L.A. I will pay 2,500 dollars for the first two weeks of work. If it takes longer than that, we can discuss terms at that point. Would that be something that you're interested in?"

"Well, Mr. Banks—"

"Jay—" I interrupted, giving her a taste of her own medicine.

"Of course, Jay. As you know I am not a professional. I did this on my own. You should hire someone more qualified than myself."

"Well, from the looks of things, you've done an outstanding job and I would appreciate your help."

"Since you put it that way, Mr. Ban— Jay, it would be my pleasure."

Eight

Chapter 8

Traci

Out of nowhere he pops up here, in my office. Coincidentally with a L.A. office. Sounds funny to me. But whatever. If he is willing to pay me $2500 for color schemes, plush pillows and furniture, (none of which I have to pay for, just suggest) I'm all for it.

"Since we are going to be working together, maybe we should address the tension between us." "Tension, there isn't any tension."

"Ok, maybe not tension. More like the elephant in the room. I hope this will not be uncomfortable for us at all."

"No, definitely not. To be honest, it was dropped back in Jamaica. I didn't think I would see you again. I thought we would handle all of our business over the phone and zoom meeting since the last I knew you were a New York resident. But it is what it is! I am a professional and I will handle myself

Chapter 8

as such."

He seemed to be taken back by my honesty. He leaned back in his chair and stroked his goatee with his hands before replying. "I understand. Since we're being honest, I didn't expect to see you again either. My assistant notified me you were nearby and I should stop by to let you know of our plans. Needing your help, if you were interested. The L.A. project was in the works before I even met you. I'm glad that you think all my movements revolved around you, it's cute. Nevertheless, glad we can remain professionals. It was nice talking with you Ms. Traci, I will be in touch."

He gathered himself and walked out. How cocky of him. Cute? I'm grown, I am not cute nor do I act it. I'm glad we could get past this. I couldn't see myself with him anyway, the way he just acted. Who am I kidding? It made him look finer than he did the day I met him. All of this just made things more difficult. Not only will I be working with him but I will be working with him consistently for the next two weeks. Jesus, please take the wheel.

Jay

Was there any doubt that I wouldn't be able to handle myself professionally? Who did she even think she was? The Queen of Sheba. That everybody would tremble in her presence. Yield to her every beck and call. Sheeeet. I'm mother-fucking Joseph Elliot Banks. And she is not the first and surely will not be the last. She is replaceable, dispensable. It will be nothing for me to move on. Right? *****

As I pulled up to Ma'dear's house, I noticed she was out on the patio. Buying her a house in L.A. was one of the first things I did when the plans of the location were in works. I knew there was a possibility that I would stay, so bringing her made it more definite.

She was always calm in the midst of my storms. I had always taken care of my mama and Ma'Dear since I started the business. When my mom got sick, Ma'Dear was always the one to help me press on after her death. I was in a bad place. Leading me to dive even more into work, that and medical expenses.

Not only did she help clear my mind, she had the best fried chicken a man could ask for. Every Thursday, that was her speciality. Fried chicken, String Beans, Hot Water Cornbread, Mashed Potatoes and Sweet Tea. Ma'dear was from New York herself. I never knew how she could cook, how she did, but she could put the best southern mother to shame.

"How are you doing, Ma'Dear?"

"Bout' good as I could be, baby. How about yourself?"

"I'm good, Ma'Dear. What have you been up to?"

"Oh, you know me, baby. A little bit of this, and a little of that. I picked them tomatoes from the garden for you to take. How long are you gonna be home this time?"

"I'll be home for a while, Ma'Dear. Have to look over the plans for this new location." "Oh yeah, how's that going?"

"It's going good. I just hired an interior decorator. So that should move it along quite nicely." "Is she cute?"

"Ma'am?"

"Don't ma'am me! You heard what I said. Is…she…cute?"

"Ma'Dear, I didn't even notice."

"Joseph Elliott Banks, I know you ain't bout' to sit here and lie to me 'bout not noticing if that girl was cute or not. You are a man, a grown man at that. You ain't blind nor dumb, I know you know a pretty girl when you see her. Now I'm going to ask you one mo' time, was she pretty?" "Yes ma'am, beautiful. But

Chapter 8

we can't see each other. We work together, so we're trying to keep it professional."

"Now baby, you can't let that get in your way. If things are meant to be, then they're meant to be. You can't hide from or fight destiny. If I would have done that, I would have never met your grandfather.

Just promise me one thing, if you have feelings for her you need to let her know now. Tomorrow isn't promised and you don't wanna live life with the what if's."

"Yes, ma'am."

She reached over and tapped me on the knee, "Good baby. Now let's go inside and get us something to eat. I know you are hungry."

"Yes ma'am." I replied, helping her from her seat and walking her inside the house.

*****

That night I laid in my bed, thinking, thinking about what my grandmother said. And she was right. But all I could do at this point was to play my position. And let her come to me. Only time will tell.

Chapter 9

Traci

I arrived at the Simple Touch Massage Clinic early. I thought it was earlier than everyone else since there was no one else parked outside yet. I walked inside and called out to see if anyone was there. Had to be. The doors were unlocked.

"Hello, is anybody here?" I yelled out, continuing to walk in, looking around corners to see if anyone was here.

"In here," a voice called out from a room in the back of the building. I proceeded with caution because at that moment I was unsure of who it was. I yelled out again, "Where?"

"I'm Here." He called back. The sound came from behind me. It startled me, I jumped slightly, before walking in his direction.

"My apologies, I didn't mean to startle you."

"It's ok, where's the rest of the crew." Getting straight to the point.

"Hey, they stepped out for an early lunch. They had a long

Chapter 9

day ahead of them, so they figured they would grab something early."

Finding it hard to believe and looking like it was planned, I continued on. "So what are we doing today?"

"Here are some swatches and color schemes that I plan to go with. What do you think?" Giving the samples once over, he had taste. I could tell. This would be easy and I would be out before you know it.

"I like 'em. You did a magnificent job picking them out. So tell me, what do you plan on doing with this space?"

As he explained his vision for the place, he walked me through the office.

"Even though this will be the main headquarters, we will still have a couple of spaces for massage rooms. So I will need to set those up as such. They will be more toward the front and the offices will be in the back toward to left. I want the massage rooms to have a personal feeling as well as the office spaces."

He talked with the same passion. You could tell that he really cared and loved what he did. He felt about his business the same way I did about mine. It was kind of attractive. Trevor and I never shared that same drive. I had to work for everything that I got; it was like everything was given to him. Since he was the basketball star. Everyone catered to him. I never received that kind of treatment, and I could tell Jay was the same way.

We continued to go through the layout. The crew slowly returned. Giving me a calm sense that we were no longer by ourselves. They brought food for us all to eat, from a popular burger spot nearby. "I hope you don't mind, I ordered a little something for you. I knew you were on your way and I wasn't sure if you picked up something to eat on the way."

He was right; I neglected to eat on the way here. I was so

nervous; I forgot to. Never understanding the reason, it just happens whenever I'm in his presence. It wasn't just the fact that we slept together either. It seemed so much more. But because of the way things were, it had to be this way. "You seemed like a burger and fries type girl. So that's what I got you. I hope you don't mind." "Is that a double bacon ranch burger?"

"Yes, ma'am. I've had it twice, and it's my favorite."

"Mine too."

"With a Dr. Pepper," we said in unison.

I blushed and bowed my head, hiding my smile and embarrassment.

"Why do you hide your face whenever you smile? It's beautiful."

"It's a nervous thing. I've always done it."

"Well, you shouldn't. So tell me a little about yourself. Where did you grow up? What made you want to go into the business that you did?"

"Well, my aunt and uncle raised me since I was young. My mother is a recovering drug addict, so they took me in. I was born and raised in Hawthorne. I lived there until college. Went to UCLA, graduated and started Already Booked, the rest is history." Trying to keep it as short as possible. He didn't need to know my entire life story. "What about yourself?" Changing the subject from me to him. "Born and raised in New York, lived there all my life. Started my business at 22, as a trade to get me off the streets. As weird as it sounds, I used to give my mom and Ma'Dear massages when I was younger and I enjoyed it. So instead of running the streets, I worked hard to make a business out of it. And here I am, a couple of hundred dollars richer and multiple locations in the works."

How modest, a couple of hundred dollars. They estimate his

Chapter 9

net worth at a quarter million dollars, and that was before the expansion. After everything was said and done, there isn't any telling where it would be.

"A true success story."

"I guess you would say so. I would just say it's a true story of hard work and dedication. Like yourself." I blushed again, "Well it looks like we should get back to work. What should we do next?" "I know there is a business furniture place in Central L.A. off of La Brea, that I wanted to check out. Do you mind coming with me to check it out?"

"Of course, I'll meet you down there. What's the address?"

"Now, Traci. Don't be silly, We can take my car. It makes little sense to drive in two cars to the same place just to come back. After we're finished, I'll bring you back and we'll call it a day." "If you insist."

"I do."

As I gathered my things, he motioned to his employees that he would be back and to let him know if they needed anything. We walked outside, he pointed me toward a 2020 Yukon Denali Truck with 22" chrome finished rims, black with cream interior. Of course, this would be his truck, it seemed like something that would fit him.

As we approached the car, he followed me toward the passenger side and reached to open the car door for me. I caught a whiff of his cologne. He smelled of coffee, sage and amber; a real masculine scent. I closed my eyes to take it all in. He smelled so good! Keep it together, Traci. Keep it together. "Thanks," I said, as he closed the door.

It was a beautiful day, sad that I spent it working. But because of my newfound freedom, mama had to make the bacon.

Love Interrupted

Jay

We arrived at the furniture store and looked around. She saw a couple of things she liked, that would fit the decor and as did I. But we agreed to continue our search until we found something better. She mentioned a spot that we should check out tomorrow, that would probably be better. We agreed and made our way back to the office.

We drove in awkward silence. I broke it with the sultry sounds of Ledisi. Her song, "Anything For You", played on the radio.

"Oh, I loved this song," she said as she swayed and snapped her fingers.

"Oh, yeah. Me too. Another thing we have in common."

"Yeah."

Needless to say, the rest of the ride was smooth. Music will always be a great icebreaker.

* * *

The next couple of weeks passed by quickly, quicker than I would have liked. I would have enjoyed having spent more time with her, but such as life. I was prepared to take my time and let things happen organically or if she moved first.

I had been gone the last couple of dates, get my apartment ready. I had taken time off to get things situated.

My grandmother had a huge backyard behind the house that I purchased for her. So instead of buying a whole other apartment or house. I had a team build me a tiny house in the back. That way I could be close and wouldn't have to be worried about her too much if I were further away. Traci was already here. I wasn't surprised since the beginning she had taken this

Chapter 9

all hands on. I admired her dedication.

She was gathering her thing to leave. I called out to her, "Was it that time already?" "Yes Sir," she replied. As she continues to make her way to the door. "How is everything with the apartment going?"

"Everything is great, they should be finished tomorrow."

"Glad to hear. I guess you will finally be about to call yourself an official Los Angeles resident." "I guess so."

"Well, alright. I will be back in the morning, same time. See you then?"

"Yeah, tomorrow. Have a great evening."

"You as well."

Traci

After leaving Jay's office, I figured I would treat myself to a movie. The Gemini, had been playing at the AMC theaters. I have been waiting to check it out. They had a 7:25 showing; I figured I would grab me something to eat, get in a little retail therapy and it would be just the right time for the credit to start. So I did just that.

I first went to Chick-Fil-A. Purchased a Sandwich combo and set down in the food court area. "Traci, Traci, is that you?" I heard a voice call me from a distance. It was a sound of a familiar voice but I prayed to God that he wouldn't come any closer or I could hide my face well enough for him to not think it was me.

"Traci."

Shit, it was him. It was Trevor. I had done well to avoid him since our breakup.

How and why did I have to slip up today?

"Why are you calling out my name, like we're friends?" The

horrible thing about being in the city, is that there's always a possibility you would run into someone that you know. I thought I had done so well, but today just had to prove me wrong.

"Come on now, is that the way you should talk to the man you were supposed to spend forever with?" "No, maybe not. But it is the way you should talk to a lowdown dirty dog, who cheated on you?" "That was forever ago, I've changed."

"Trevor, it had only been six months. It was impossible to do that kind of change that you need in six months."

"You know you miss me. I know I miss you. Traci, it's been long enough. We could just continue where we left off, start again, whatever you need."

Was this dude delusional? Has he lost his mind? Well, I should have known he had. Especially after the night, I tried to knock his head completely off.

"Where we left off, start over….You must really be full of yourself. You make a fool of for as long as you have and you expect for me just to take you back. Just like that?"

"Well, yeah. I was your first. You love me."

"You thought you were my first, didn't you?" He stared at me with a look of confusion and hurt. It was a low blow. I knew it hurt him, I could feel that it did. "Well, you enjoy the rest of your day," I said, wrapping up my trash and standing up to leave.

Be I could make an exit, he grabbed my arm. I could feel my blood pressure rise. I gave him a stern look, as I snatched my arm away.

"I thought you the last time, you put your hands on me again and I will kill you." "I just wanted to let you know one thing before you go. Kayla is pregnant and will apply for

Chapter 9

unemployment, just a heads up. Since you fired her, she has been out of work due to her condition. So she will need some incoming money for her finances."

My jaw dropped. Not only did he cheat on me, but he got this bitch pregnant and begged for me to come back. All in one sitting. This narcissist prick. But as my mother would always say, if you can't do anything else, kill them with kindness.

"That's good to hear, Trevor. I hope everything works out for you and her. You guys deserve one another. Takes a creep to know one."

That was the last word. After he had sat there and stepped on my heart for the last time. I could not allow him to follow up with anything else.

Way to ruin my entire evening. I chose to just grab a couple of things from stores within where I was and call it the day. Just that conversation alone had taken so much out of me. I would have to catch the movie another time. On the way home, I guess I'll just pick me up some Ben and Jerry's, curl up on the couch and watch T.V. till I pass out.

Damn.

Ten

Chapter 10

Jay

It was the beginning of what looked like a great day. The contractor made the finishing touches on my house that morning, and I could move in this afternoon. No more hotel nights or sleeping in my grandmother's guest room. I had a place to call home. For the first time in a while. I called Traci to get a second opinion and maybe some suggestions. I went inside to check on Ma'Dear. She was preoccupying herself baking my favorite, her world famous sweet potato pie. Before I knew it, there was a car pulling up in the driveway. It took her no time to get here. She must live close by. I met her outside, welcoming her to my humble abode.

"Beautiful," she said, looking around, taking in all the scenery. "You must have someone here that loves gardening, they did a great job. Everything looks amazing, very welcoming. Almost Zen ." "Yes, she is a very special woman." Traci looked at me

Chapter 10

unhinged with a slight bit of confusion. I interrupted her glare, "My Grandmother, she stays here."

"I thought you said you lived here."

"I do, follow me." I guided her to the back of the house. She was at a loss for words. The contractors had done an outstanding job. They laid sod, the concrete walkways leading from the driveway to the house, the house to Ma'dear house, flowers and planters, plus lawn chairs with tables and an umbrella. She continued to walk around speechless.

"This is beautiful, Jay!"

"Wait until you see the inside!" Directing her into the house. Entering the doors, she came into the living room area. It was a couch that turned into a bed to your right, a kitchenette on the side. And on the left it said to the small bathroom slash laundry room. It was just the right amount of space for me.

It was basically the same amount of space I would get staying in any hotel. Not only that, but it would cut down on hotel expenses. I finally had a spot to call my own. Looking over to her, trying to find approval, "So how'd I do?"

"You didn't need my help. You did great all on your own."

"My personal space is different. I know what I like. But a place for everybody, it's good to have someone else's opinion."

"Great job," she said in a melancholy tone.

"What's wrong."

"Just thinking about me and my living situation. Moving from my own space to a place that I have to share with my best friend. Not that it's bad, it's just staying in your own place makes me want my own."

"It will come. Just be patient."

"You're right, it will come. It's just been a long week. I'm looking forward to the weekend. So I can relax."

"You know what always gets me in a better mood, when I'm feeling down. Some of Ma Dear's Sweet Potato Pie."

"Oh yeah! Well, let's just see about that! Then after that we can go to the office and I'll show you another surprise that will brighten your day even more."

"Word, ok. Let's hurry up then!" directing her toward the house. Ma'Dear was in the kitchen. Cleaning up after baking, when she looked up at us.

"Ma'Dear, I would like you to meet Traci. Traci, Ma'Dear."

"Nice to meet you, ma'am."

"Hey baby, nice meeting you," Ma'Dear said as she sat down at the table in the kitchen. "Gotta sit down and rest. It feels like I've been on my feet all day. You hungry, baby? I got some smothered chicken, rice and broccoli on the stove."

"Yes, ma'am. You know it! But I bought Traci in here because she didn't believe that you had the best sweet potato pie in the whole world," I said with excitement. Fixing my plate, while carrying on the conversation.

"Well, baby. I don't know about all that, but I'm glad you like it."

"The most humble person I know." I said as I leaned over to whisper to Traci. "Hey baby, do me a favor. After you eat, clean the kitchen up for Ma'Dear would you? I'ma go in here and catch my stories. Nice meeting you, Traci. Hope to see you again!"

"Yes, ma'am. Nice meeting you too."

We sat down, enjoyed our food, made small talk and cleaned the kitchen together. Traci really enjoyed Ma'dear's cooking. Said she hadn't had a meal like that in a long time. It also seemed to lift her spirits, I was glad.

Chapter 10

Traci

We arrived at his downtown location, and he opened the door to let me out, being the gentleman he always was.

"I hope you like everything. I based everything on the swatches that were given. If there is anything that you would like to change, please let me know. I want you to be honest. This is your space, so I want to make sure it's tailored to you and your brand."

"I'm sure, I will love it."

He opened the door and let me in first, then he walked it. Silence fell between us as he walked to the office doors and surveyed the building. His jaw dropped.

At that point, I wasn't sure if he was out of praise or astonishment. He continued to walk around, while I stood in one place. Waiting for him to respond. "Well?" I said breaking the silence. "It's amazing, everything is amazing. I can't believe you did all this."

"Well, it wasn't me all by myself. Lisa put in a couple of pointers and the other staff as well. The rest was simple after that. Glad you like it."

"Like would be an understatement. This is great."

He hugged me; I shifted and pulled away. The look that appeared on his face made me regret it. "It was just a friendly hug. I meant nothing by it. I just—"

"No need to explain."

He reached in his pocket to retrieve an envelope. "Here," he said, stretching his hand to give it to me. I took the envelope and opened it. Inside was a check for $15,000. With a confused look on my face, "What is this for?"

"Consider it a thank you gift."

"Thank you, for what?"

"For a job well done. You saved us a lot of money."

"Oh well, I was just doing my job. I can't accept this."

"Traci, please. We'll be doing a lot of work together. Consider this the first of many. So let's look forward to that. And no worries, the hugs, won't ever happen again."

Damn.

I didn't respond. The look on his face I knew all too well. Hurt.

Jay

Tonight was the company's celebratory function. A party to celebrate being in business for the past ten years, the expansion to Jamaica, and the office opening up in L.A. It was a night of great accomplishments. Definitely a night that I had looked forward to after the disappointment earlier. Not that I expected anything, but I damn sure didn't expect her to be so standoffish. The way she treated me, you would have thought I was a stranger off the street. I wouldn't have ever expected her to act that way. But I guess that's what I got for thinking otherwise.

The car picked me up at 6:30 pm on the dot. The party didn't start until 7:00 pm. I had more than enough time to get there, granted that it was only fifteen minutes away.

When I arrived, everything was in full swing. The music was playing, filling the space as the entire staff dressed to the nines in their, what looked to be, Sunday's Best. Not only was the place filled with staff but also the whose, who of Hollywood. Lisa must have put them all up to this. I was never made aware of who was on the guest list, but I truly appreciated them for making the effort.

I was never one for a large gathering. But I wanted to take the time to thank the staff for all their hard work and continue

Chapter 10

efforts to build the brand. Making it what it was today. I wanted to show them that their hard work had not gone without notice.

With all that being said, I reached for a cocktail from a passing waiter and mingled amongst the crowd to calm my nerves. I could feel that they were getting the best of me.

"Aye yo, Jay!"

I looked up to see Ant yelling across the room as he walked up to approach me. At that moment, I was glad to see a familiar face. Bringing my 10 to a 5.

"Hey, Ant. Thanks for coming."

"You know I wouldn't miss this for anything in the world. Congratulations, again kid! This place looks amazing."

"That's the same thing I said when I saw it! Everything worked out perfectly." "Oh yeah, give me the number to your designer so I can have them hook some things up for me." "Yeah, I don't know if you could have this one's number, playa."

"Oh yeah, why not?"

"It's Traci."

"Traci? Oh the girl you all hung up on?"

"All hung up? I am not all hung up on that girl!"

"Oh you're not, huh? When's the last time you had a date? Hell when's the last time you got you some? And bumping uglies with 'Traci,' doesn't count. I swear you're changing right before my eyes. It's like I don't even know you anymore. The Jay I used to know would have been on to the next. No questions. I don't know who this Joseph person is."

"I've just been focused."

"Yeah, focused ... riiighhhtt. I'ma let you tell it."

Before I could open my mouth to speak, we were interrupted.

"Hello, Mr. Banks. Thanks for the invite." Nat said, reaching out for a handshake.

"Glad you two could make it." I replied, catching a glance at Traci, before Nat continued talking. "It's an exceptional turn out! I think I saw Larenz Tate over there. I think I should make friends." "Ahem," Ant cut in, trying to make his presence known. He whispered, "Aren't you going to introduce me?"

Ah, yes. Traci and Nat, this is my friend and brother, Ant."

"Pleased to make your acquaintance ladies," he reached for each of their hands and gave them a gentle kiss.

"The pleasure is all mine." Nat said, as Traci nudged her in embarrassment.

"Hey, Nat. Would you like to join me at the bar for a drink?"

"I would love to! Let's go."

I can't believe he just left me like that. I should have known. He's been trying to get me to hook him up with Nat since I told him that Traci had a single girlfriend. Such a piranha. He smelled the blood in the water and took his bite. I can't be mad. As beautiful as Nat was, I would have taken my chance too. If I wasn't so tied up with her best friend.

"You look amazing, Traci. Thanks again for coming"

"You're not too shabby yourself there, Mr. Banks. And I wouldn't have missed this for anything. Congratulations again. Listen, I apologize for the way I acted earlier. I didn't mean it. I've just been going through a lot lately. I shouldn't have taken that out on you."

"No you were right. I should respect your wish and remain professional. I never want you to feel uncomfortable."

"You didn't. It was just unexpected. And again, I apologize."

"No apologies, necessary. But forgive me again for mentioning that you look absolutely stunning in that dress. Making me wish I could be the one to take it off when everything was said and done. But, strictly business, right? I hope you have a good

Chapter 10

evening. Thanks again for coming." I said with a wink and walked into the crowd. The look she gave, I knew she instantly felt every word of that last statement. *Good!*

Traci

Damn. Now why did he have to go say something like that? Leaving me all… open.

Snapping me from a stalker's glare, Nat tapped me on my shoulder. "Earth to Traci?"

"Girl, stop!"

"Don't girl stop me. You're the one looking like you want to rip that man's clothes off with your eyes. I still don't know what the big deal is. You act like coworkers don't sleep with other coworkers all the time. And besides, you don't even work for the same company. You won't see each other every day, and y'all have ya'll own shit. If somebody has a problem with it, they can see themselves out. We are our own bosses, we make our own rules."

She was right.

"But regardless, I never want to be mentioned as one who got to where they were because they slept their way to get there."

"Please, where is he gonna take you, girl? I'm just saying, what is he, the president? Are you trying to be first lady? Who gives a fuck what people say? My mama always told me, 'If they ain't fucking me, or paying my bills, I could give a fuck what they think or say.' Words I live by to this day and so should you. If anything or anybody stands in the way of your happiness, Fuck 'em. Period!" "I'm glad that you can live life so carefree."

"You got to go for it girl or you'll never be happy. Especially living up to someone else's expectations. That's where ya mama got you all messed up. But that is something for another night. Have fun girl and do you. Be carefree, if only for once."

I needed to start living for myself and caring less about what others had to say.

Eleven

Chapter 11

Traci

It was the day after the party. It was truly a beautiful event. It kind of made me jealous to see all of Jay's accomplishments. It was sort of bittersweet. Reminding me of the what ifs. If I would have never gotten tangled up with Trevor and his Real Housewives drama, I would have been further along with my career. But I had to keep reminding myself there was no use crying over spilled milk. It would only make me bitter and full of regret. Like my mother, I refuse to live my life that way. I was going to keep pushing and look forward to the future. All of this was just the drive I needed to work harder and get more done.

I sat at the bay window in the kitchen as I collected my thoughts. Here I was trying to get past the hurt of a past relationship, dealing with feelings of a present. Not that it still hurt me about what had happened. It was just that I wanted to have my business intact. How do people juggle between business and personal? And do I really want the experience of watching the two collide? I had no one to talk this over with. I already knew of Nat's stance on things. And I knew that my mother would be no help in the situation. If only my Nana was here. She was always my voice of reason. I would always come to her when I couldn't decide on my own. Remembering my Nana, made me remember the time I spent with Jay's grandmother and him missing his mother as well. My grandmother practically raised me until she passed and I went to go stay with my aunt and uncle.

My mother has always been an absentee parent. Losing my father to the streets. You could say on that date I lost my mother too. My mother spent her time in and out of rehab. I know she tries to do better, but once that monkey is on your back, it's a hard thing to shake.

I guess that's what makes me so determined. Determined not to fail, to not be like my mother. To make my Nana proud. And I didn't want no or nobody to stand in the way of that.

"So you gonna sit there all day moping?" Nat called out, walking into that kitchen. Breaking me from my stupor.

"I'm not moping, just thinking."

"Well, don't think too long. We still have a lot to do today. Finalization for this weekend itineraries are to be done and turned and the plans for our trip to Atlanta are to be made. So if you would please ma'am, get yourself together so we can get to work."

"Ok, ok, ok. I swear a sista can't get a moment of peace without you being all down my throat about work."

"You right, cause you are always the one complaining. OMG, I wish I was further ahead than this, I wish I was that. Stop

Chapter 11

crying 'bout it and be about it. I am just trying to help you get to where you want to be. So don't get mad when I push you."

"I'm not mad. And your absolutely right"

"I know I am, you need a friend like me."

"On another note, speaking about friends? What was up with you and Jay's friend?" "Jay's Friend?" She made a face like she didn't know who I was talking about.

"Yes, Jay's Friend."

"Who Ant? Oh, girl, it was nothing. We just sat, talked, and danced. He was fine, wasn't he?" "You know he was. So...."

"So nothing. I mean, we'll see where it goes. Why are you asking? You wanna set up a double date?" "NO! You know I don't have the time or the headspace for that. I can't... I don't even know that after all we've been through so far does he even still like me like that." Lying through my teeth, I knew that he did. But the question was really was I ready.

"Girl, are you crazy, blind and deaf? He's been giving you all the signs since the beginning. To this day he still can't keep his eyes off of you and you're gonna sit up there and tell me you haven't noticed." I couldn't lie to my best friend. It always seemed like she knew me better than I knew myself. "What do you expect me to do, just walk up to him and pour my heart out? Like a love story or something. Oh Jay, I love you and I wanna spend the rest of my life with you." Shit. Why did I have to open my big mouth?

"Oohh girl, I knew it. You can't hide that shit from me! It was written all over your grill. That was the primary reason you were hiding behind all this work stuff. It had nothing to do with business. You were just too scared to admit you had feelings and you don't wanna get hurt again." Letting out a vast sigh, "Why do women have to be such emotional creatures? We wear our hearts on our sleeves vulnerable for someone to break it."

"But that's life, girl. We live every day, taking chances. That's all it is, one big chance. And you'll never know unless you take the leap. But I'm not going to continue giving out this good free love advice. We're going to finish these itineraries so you can take them down to your man. And hopefully while you're down there you can get you some. Or, should I say, some more?"

* * *

Nat and I finished up all the work for Mr. Banks. It took no time at all. Within minutes, I was in my car driving down the 405 to his office. Yet another beautiful day in Southern California, and I spent the majority of it in the house. I have got to find better things to do with my time than to spend my time overthinking.

I pulled up to his office and realized that nobody was there. That odd, it's a weekend. Someone is always here, working on something. Especially Jay. I tried calling him and he didn't answer. Another thing that was out of the ordinary. He always answered my calls.

I gathered my nerves as I approached Jay's doorbell. And before I lost my cool, my body took over, and I pressed the button. I think I pressed the doorbell so hard; I think the neighbors came outside to see who it was.

"Hey, eh what are you doing here? I mean, is everything ok?" he stared at me with a look of bewilderment. I barely recognized him. I always saw Jay dressed in jeans, slacks, polos or dressed shirts. Never tattered basketball shorts, jersey and an ungroomed beard. I could tell today was an off day, I glad

Chapter 11

that I came back to check on him. Hopefully, the feeling was reciprocated. "Um, yeah. I didn't mean to bother you, but I had your final plans and itineraries for your employees. I went by the office to drop them off and you weren't there. Which I thought was unusual. So I wanted to make sure you were ok."

"Oh yeah, so you were worried about your boy, huh?"

I bowed my head, so he didn't see my expression. He took his finger and bought my face back up to meet his. "It's ok, I won't hold it against you."

At that moment, he looked behind him and returned his glance to me with a weary look. "I'm so sorry, I hope I'm not interrupting anything?" I never even thought about the fact that he could have somebody over. We had never discussed our relationships outside of work. Even after all this time.

"No, why would you think anything like that? My place, it's just a mess. I wasn't expecting company." "Well, I will leave you to continue what you were doing and I'll—" before I could continue my statement, he stepped to the side. Widening the space between him and the door, letting me in. "I was just about to sit down and eat. You hungry?"

"Famished."

"Well, I guess you came at the right time. I have taken out and ordered more than enough. Join me." "I would love to."

We ate in silence. After each bite, I caught a glance of him. This man was truly beautiful. It was almost like I was seeing him for the first time. He seemed different. A Lot different from the cocky, pompous businessman he was on a day to day basis. It was almost as if all of that was a safeguard to hide who he really was, and I was seeing it all for the first time.

As we continued our meal, I noticed a picture on the wall. It was of a beautiful woman. She had long black hair, eyes and complexion the same as his. It was a picture of her walking along a beach. You could see the waves and behind it rests a breath-taking sunset.

"It was her first time in L.A. before she passed. She wanted to come here after all the stories she heard about Hollywood, Celebrities and beaches. She wanted to experience it all before she was to leave this earth. I had to make sure I made that wish come true."

I looked up from my plate with so much remorse. And before I could part my lips, he said, "Breast Cancer. She passed away from breast cancer just two years ago. Two years ago today. It's always a rough day for me. So I just spend it by myself. I never wanted anyone to see me in this state. At least not until today."

Not until today? I was speechless. Why would he want to share a moment so sacred with me? We barely knew each other.

"I'm so sorry, you have told me countless amounts of time that you want to remain professional, but when I'm with you… I just can't. Every time I'm around you, it just brings me back to the first time. My mind wanders back to your lips, your hips and how it felt to be inside you. And I know now is not the time to express such, but I just couldn't go on another day without letting you know that I care about you."

As he made his confession, I could feel my bud swell. I've never had a man profess his feelings for me. He was so sincere, so kind, so gentle. I saw his sincerity in how he looked at me. It was almost like his eyes were the windows to his soul and it was fixed and craved me.

"I know that you have been through a lot with your past relationship, but that's not me. Women have raised me my entire life, and I know how to treat a good one when I see one. I don't want to jump into anything or I don't want an answer to

Chapter 11

anything today. I just felt that too much time has passed. Life is too short, for regrets. And you were not a regret I will take.

I could feel my eyes water. This man sat here and bared it all. And all I could do was sit with a confused look on my face and wonder why? The wasted seven year relationship left me feeling unwanted and unloved. And in just a couple month's time, this man was willing to risk it all. Risk it all on damaged goods.

He reached for my face, palming it in his hand. "Don't you know you are worth it? You are worth more than I could ever give you. But I am willing to try. Try to give you everything and more. I have feelings for you, Traci Elenore Carter."

I damn near fainted. He reached out to catch me and when I opened them; I saw the most genuine, loving person I've ever seen in my life.

"Are you alright?" He stared at me with a look of concern.

"I'm, I'm just—"

His lips pressed against mine. It was almost like time stood still. My stomach filled with butterflies and my heart raced faster. My legs grew weak. Likely, I was in his arms and he held me from my temporary paralysis. It was almost as if he was in a dream. But no dream had ever felt this good. I could only focus on the soft touch of his lips as he scooped me up to rest me on my feet. Still in a haze, I stood with my eyes closed, fighting to maintain my balance... trying to control my staggered breathing.

When I looked up at his face, I could see a trail from where a tear had fallen. He held me close, his immense body engulfed my small frame, as he whispered in my ear. "I'll never hurt you."

Jay

And I meant every word. The cat and mice game we continued to play grew tiresome. I didn't want to play anymore games. I wanted her to be mine. Regardless of the work situation. In my mind, I had already dismissed the feelings of what people had to say. This was our lives, and the feeling we shared was beyond real and too intense to deny. For the rest of the evening she laid there, in my bed, in my arms. It's the most peace I've endured in a long time.

Twelve

Chapter 12

Jay

...one year earlier

I don't know why Ant felt it was necessary to be involved in my sex life but he evidently did. He had set me up with a blind date between me and someone from his office, that he seemed to think that I was so perfect for. Blind dates always seemed like just a set up, a set up for failure. Either they would be ugly, the two of you would have nothing in common or the whole vibe would be off period. I had no time for a relationship. I was successful, handsome and hardworking. I could get a woman at any time. Getting them was not the problem, but keeping them probably would be a harder task. I wasn't interested in putting on the charade of getting to know anyone new, let alone dating. I was beginning to think the life that I was living would leave me alone. I always wanted to be in a relationship. But the question was always with whom? And how would I ever find the time? I was focused. Focused on my business and my family.

My mother was going through her second round of chemotherapy, so a date was far from my mind. But I could understand where he was coming from. He wanted to take my mind off of it, off of everything. I appreciated him for that.

It was 7:30 pm when I arrived at the Coofee's that Saturday. I surveyed the area to make sure that no one that looked like my date had arrived before I could get a chance to. It was always my logic that if you arrived at the location before the set time, that you had the upper hand. Where to sit, get your drink to relax the first date jitters and calm your nerves. It was the person coming in that would have to experience the initial shock. Find the table, approach the person and sit with the stranger. Being already seated, I could see her before she saw me.

7:45 pm rolled around, I sat there still waiting for the mystery lady to make her grand entrance. I took it upon myself to order some appetizers, I didn't want this whole evening to be a complete waste. Plus a brotha had to eat.

I can't believe it! Didn't Ant tell her my pet peeve is when people are not on time. But that was my problem, I expect people to be like it. And that would be hard for a common person to achieve. *Remain Calm. She'll be here. But if 8:00 rolls around and she's still not here, I'm leaving.*

7:55 pm in comes this attractive mocha skinned woman. She stood 5'7, an excellent complement to my 6'2 stature. She wore a mustard color wrap around dress with heels to match. The dress draped off her shoulders accentuating her cleavage, which undoubtedly caught my eye making it hard for me not to stare. But I made sure that my gaze was discreet.

I motioned for her as she began to walk closer to our table.

Chapter 12

As she came closer, I could only help to acknowledge the beauty that was displayed at the door was a far cry from that up close and personal.

I got up from my seat to greet her and went in for the hug. Her scent was enticing. She smelled like floral tones and lavender, it was relatively calming. "Hi, Joseph. Nice to meet you." "Hi, Joseph. Angela."

"Angela, that is a beautiful name," I said, as she sat in the chair as I returned it to its normal position. "Thank you, I was named after my mother's favorite actress. It fit well because my last name is Barnett."

"Oh, wow. I like that. So tell me a little bit about yourself."

"I work for an accounting firm in Manhattan. I have been with the company for a little over four years. I've just received my master's in Accounting opening things up to either a promotion and a higher paying job. I have no kids and I've never been married. How about yourself?" "Straight shooter, I like that. I own a massage clinic with various locations. I completed my Master's in Business Administration over two years ago. I have no children and I've never been married either." "Various locations, huh? So you travel?

Was that all she heard? "Yeah, I travel a little bit. I like going to different places from time to time. See new things, enjoy new stuff."

"Wow, that's amazing. Jersey was the furthest I've gone. Maybe you can suggest a great place I can go when I get the chance."

"Yeah, I can certainly do that."

The night was filled with enjoyable conversation. I was glad I came out. It reminded me of how, even if I was by myself or in the company of an attractive young lady, I need to go out more. One drink turned into two, and two turned into three and by then I could tell that she was a little tipsy. She started to call herself an Uber, but in her state I wanted to make sure she got home safely. These crowd share drivers nowadays are too suspicious.

We finished our drinks and our meal and called it a night. I called for the waiter, paid the tab and we made our way out the door.

We stepped out into the night air, it was a little brisk outside. I took off my jacket and rested it on her shoulders, shielding her from the gentle breeze.

"Mind if I smoke?" she asked, pulling out a marijuana filled cigarette from her purse. "No, I don't mind at all."

"Do you smoke?"

"On occasion, when I need to clear my mind from the outside noise."

"It helps me calm my nerves."

"Why, do I make you nervous?" I said, inching closer to her, invading her privacy bubble. I could feel the tension between us as I noticed the hairs standing on the back of her neck. It was either she was still cold or I was right. She quickly lit the joint and put it between her lips. Inhaling twice and handing it to me. I did the same and passed it back, leaving an open invitation for a continued rotation to take place. At that moment I knew that I had to find a way out of this situation before it turned into something I wasn't sure I was ready for.

Twenty minutes had passed and we arrived at her house. I could feel the combination of the foreign inhabitants taking over my body. And I was damn sure that if she was already in an impaired state when we left, she had to be hella bent now. The plan was to drop her off and leave. But I should have known

Chapter 12

her and my dick had other plans.

Walking her up to the door, watching her ass sashay back and forth, made my stick hard. *I knew I should have watched her from the car. Look we're just going up there and coming right back down. No funny stuff.*

We reached her apartment door. She fumbled around for her keys in her purse until she came across them, unlocked and opened the door. "Well, I had a wonderful evening. Hope that we can do it again sometime—" Before I knew, her lips collided with mine. Leaving no space in between us and her tongue holding my mouth captive. This was exactly what I had been trying to avoid. The point of no return.

Shit.

Now.

Traci laid in my bed, with the face of a sleeping angel. Sprawled across the bed, as if she was getting the best rest she'd ever received in her life. No lies to be told, she has made me feel the best I'd felt in a long time. It was almost like the Lord above sent her here to save me from myself. To save me from drowning in depression and pity. At the moment when everything felt right in the world, there always has to be a moment when something just had to go wrong.

The devil always finds a way to disrupt best laid plans.

I was in the kitchen fixing breakfast when I heard the phone ring. Putting my wrong from the counter, I realized it from a number from Jersey. Of all places? Who could be calling me from there. Wishing I would have let it go to voicemail, I answered it.

"Hello."

"Hello, Yes. May I speak to Joseph." Whole Government, must be a bill collector. *"Yes, this is he."*

"Yes, uh I don't know if you remember me but this is Angela, Angela Barnett."

"Yeah, of course. Of course I remember you. Yeah hey, how are you doing?"

"Good, good. Considering..." Considering?

"Mmm, I'm sorry to hear that. But I haven't talked to you in a while. What's been going on?" I don't know why, but I felt like some bad news was coming.

"I don't know of an easier way to say this..." Ahh shit here it comes, brace for impact. *"After the last time we had sex, something happened. Something happened resulting in me getting pregnant. I had the baby about a month ago. His name is Tyler. I thought you would want to meet him, since he's yours."*

Silence.

I looked toward my room, toward my bed toward her. I didn't care about the situation. All I cared about right at the moment was how it was going to make the woman in the bed feel. How I had just professed my feelings to her and now almost literally in the same breath, I have to turn around and tell her that I might have a kid out of the blue. With a woman that's not even her. *Shit.*

"Hello?"

"I'm sorry, I was just caught off guard."

"Yeah, I'm sorry. I've tried to reach you at your location in Jackson Heights but you were never available."

"Yeah shortly after we hooked up, I moved to California."

"Oh wow! That's quite a move."

"Yeah.

"Yeah, well I just thought I would take the time to make sure that you knew."

"Well yeah, um, I have your number so uh..I'll be sure to give you

Chapter 12

a call back so we can discuss this further. I'm kind of in the middle of something right now. But I'll be sure to hit you up." Silence.

"Oh well, please be sure that you do.

"Well, it was nice talking to you. Have a good one."

"You as well—" and before she could say anything else, I hung up the phone.

I stood there. I stood there for a long while. Trying to get myself together. Collect my thoughts, make calculations. WHAT THE ENTIRE FUCK!!!!????!!!! How did you do this to yourself Joseph? There wasn't any kind of way she could be pregnant. AIN'T NO FUCKING WAY!!!! I strapped up right. Trying hard to recall the night's events. But my memory was more than cloudy, remembering the drinks we had after getting back to her apartment. *Shit.* I did it to myself. Why didn't she tell me sooner? Why wait until now? How does this make me look…to her? Snapping back to, I realized my eggs started to burn. I glance back into the room. She was still in the same position I left her and thank God. All of this with Angela would have to be handled separately and carefully. I would have to make sure that everything was on the up and up before introducing her to this devastating news. Don't get me wrong, having a baby is the most precious and amazing thing to ever happen to a woman or man. But given the current circumstance, it wasn't how I wanted it to go down.

Trying to clear my head, I carried on with preparing breakfast. I placed all the food on a tray to serve it to my sleeping beauty. It was hard to believe that even when she woke up she was beautiful. I almost didn't want to wake her. Hair seemed to be in place and not one blemish on her face. It was a beautiful canvas. She was straight off of the works of Amy Sheard or even Arrington Porter. Seating the tray beside her, she gradually began to awaken.

Rubbing the sleep from her eyes, she covered her mouth in shock. "How long did I sleep? When did you have time to cook all this? And wait a minute, you can cook?" She rambled all of that off in one breath.

"If I knew you were going to be so talkative in the morning I would have let you stay asleep." I laugh as she propped herself up in the bed and gave me a nudge on the shoulder. Dismissing what I said, she grabbed her fork and took a morsel of food in her mouth. While she chewed, her eyes rolled back into her head. "Oh…My…God this is delicious. Are you sure that you didn't miss your calling?"

"My mother and grandmother made sure I knew how to get around a little bit in the kitchen. They always wanted to make sure that I knew how to feed and take care of myself. They were never too fond of eating out. So they made sure I didn't either."

"Understood. Well I know I'm enjoying every bit of it. Thank you to them both."

Traci

I couldn't even believe the night and morning I had. If you would have told me yesterday that I would whine up in the bed lying next to this man, I wouldn't have believed you. Yet alone waking up in the morning to an immaculate breakfast. And to think that I almost passed up on this beautiful surprise.

"So with everything that transpired last night, where do we go from here? We still have to work with each other, we still have to conduct ourselves in some form or fashion…" I said removing the tray from my lap and placing it to the side. Back to business as usual. Damn, Traci. You couldn't have let a great morning be just that. Had to go on with the mouth vomit.

Chapter 12

"What do you mean?" he said, with a perplexed look on his face. "We can handle this however you want to handle this. We are still at the beginning stages, so I don't want to rush. I don't want to make you uncomfortable either. So as long as I'm with you, I'll just take your lead."

I was sort of relieved. Grant it that we did just spend the evening together and he did tell me he had feelings for me and all. I almost thought he was ready to shout it out upon the rooftops. Glad he wasn't at that point. I would have to say that I was still a little confused, confused as to where this was going and how it would end if it did.

I could tell that by asking him the question that I did, not responding to him saying I love you and the lingering silence was beginning to weigh heavy on his thoughts. To break through the thick tension in the atmosphere I blurted out, "I'm sorry, I don't want to make it seem as if I don't have feelings for you, I do. I have for a while. I'm just scared, you know. I don't want to be so involved with a relationship the way I was with my ex. It was almost as if it consumed me. I couldn't focus on the things that were important to me. All of this is truly new to me. And due to the fact that you have a business yourself, I hope you can understand. I want to continue to see where this goes but I still want to…"

"I get it. It's all new to me as well. But like I said before I want to make sure that you are always comfortable. I don't want to rush into anything. Just wanted to make sure that you knew where I stood."

"Thank you, thank you for being understanding." I reached over and kissed him on his cheek. I glanced over at my watch, "Shit, I'm running late. Thank you for breakfast as well, everything was exceptional. Loved to stay and I apologize for having to eat and run but I have a lot planned for today. Call you later?" Saying all this while grabbing my things and heading for the door. "Uh, yeah. I'll talk to you then." he said unsurely and watched me in a rush. "When will I be able to see you again?"

"We'll talk about it tonight. Tonight when I call you. Thanks again." I said, kissing him and quickly making my way to my car. When I got there, I glanced up toward his apartment, he was still standing there looking at me. I gave him a wave as I got into my car and drove off.

"What the hell did you do that for? Are you crazy girl? You know damn well you didn't have anything to do that was that important today. To skip out on a man that just told you he loves you? Girl you must have that sunshine coochie! Making these niggas lose they mind over you." "Evidently not, I couldn't keep Trevor." I said as I plopped down on the couch as I continued trying to plead my case to Nat. "I don't want to be involved in yet another failed attempt at love. All I can think about is the what ifs."

Nat interjected, "Love is a chance, and so is life. If you don't take the leap you'll never know. Your gonna be the old lady with cats and the swiveled up coochie."

"Don't make me laugh, that shit isn't funny."

"Hell, I'm laughing. So it is! What are you gonna do now? You know you're scheduled to leave for Dallas this weekend. Do you plan to at least talk to him before you go?"

"Maybe I should just wait until I come back? It's already bad enough I have to go and deal with my mother. I don't want to have to worry about anything extra. I'm already confused as it is."

Thirteen

Chapter 13

Jay

Why in the hell did I put myself out there like that? I feel so stupid. She didn't even say anything. I don't even know if her feelings are reciprocated. I wish she didn't even show up at my apartment. I was in an emotional state and my emotions got the best of me. I couldn't help that it was the way I felt. But I should have just held it all back until I was sure she felt the same. I feel like a damn fool. I told her I had feelings for her.

"You told her what? Bro have you lost your mind? You never put yourself out there like that. Always make them say it first then you say it. That's why you cover yourself. Now what? What are you going to do now?"

"I don't know. I guess wait until she makes the next move."

"Yeah, I think that would be your best bet."

"Yeah, but there's more."

"There's more?"

"Yeah, you remember Angela?

"Yeah, the girl I set you up with a while back. What about her?"

"Yeah, her. She just had a kid."

"Yeah, well good for her. You saw her, what is she doing here? I know she called me a while back asking for your number. I was confused thinking she already had it. I didn't think much about it. Now she's kinda sounding stalkerish."

"Nah, she called me. Evidently the baby's mine."

"The Fuck?!?"

"That's what I said."

"How in the hell is she gonna hit you up, all outta the blue and tell you some shit like that? That was over a year ago. Why didn't she tell you when she first found out?"

"I don't know man. That's what makes everything even more difficult. First this shit with Traci, now this? How do I even tell her? I can't tell her."

"You shouldn't tell her! Not yet anyway. Not until you're sure."

"Exactly what I was thinking."

"Damn bro. You sure do have yourself in some shit!"

"I didn't plan it to be that way."

"I know bro. Damn."

"Aye, yo. I'ma holla atcha later. I'ma go to the gym and relieve some stress."

"Aight bro. Hit me up later."

"Aight, late."

I hung up. My mind raced, my thoughts were all over the place. I had to get to the bottom of all of this, and quick. After I got through talking to Ant, I decided to make the difficult call to Angela, so we can set up a time to meet and to discuss the

Chapter 13

situation at hand. After I made the arrangements for the meet up with Angela, I drove to the gym to let out my frustrations. Sex would always work in situations like this. But I guess that's what got me here in the first place. FML.

* * *

A couple of days had passed and I still haven't talked to Traci. At this point, I figured it all was a lost cause. I moved too fast and it scared her away. Just the thought of it sent a piercing pain to my heart. This is exactly why I don't get involved in relationships and rarely fall in love as it is. You're always subject to getting your heartbroken. Lesson learned. Well, at least I had something to look forward to. The possibility of having a mini me.

Angela and I have been in contact ever since I received the news. Even though it wasn't the most fitting circumstances, I figured that I would make the best of it. Not just that but to make sure that I stood up and took care of my responsibilities like a man. My mother always made sure she raised me to always do what was right.

Angela had never been to L.A. before and figured that it would be a great time to come visit. She was on maternity leave from her job so everything worked out perfectly. I arranged for her to stay at a nearby hotel since my place was too small for the three of us.

I was anxious and nervous all at the same time. Anxious about the fact that I was going to be a father for the first time and nervous about if the baby was even mine. She swore that at the time she got pregnant that I was the only one she had been with. But I had seen scenarios like this before. It was also hard to believe because I always made sure I prevented things like this from happening. I made a vow to myself that once the day came when we were to meet, I would not allow myself to get too attached. In order to avoid yet another heartbreak within the span of just a couple of months.

Angela met me at a bistro down the street from the hotel where she was staying. She was as beautiful as the first day I met her. Little had changed, she was curvier than before. And definitely not in a bad way. It seemed like all her pregnancy weight filled all the right places. As she approached the table, where I was sitting she came more into view. And so did the baby she was carrying. The baby

that was supposedly mine was snuggled up in a pouch in front of her. As she came closer, my heart raced. The moment that I loafed for over the last month since she told me, was here. I stood to my feet and removed the chair from the table so she could sit comfortably before pushing it in slightly.

"Thank you for joining me. Have you enjoyed yourself so far?"

"Haven't really done much. But it sure is beautiful out here. I can see why you like it." "Yeah, it is different. I do like it out here." Taking my attention from her to the baby she cradled in her arms.

"Allow to formally introduce the two of you. This is Tyler. Tyler Banks."

Trying to hide the dumbfounded look that came across my face. I asked, "Tyler Banks, you gave him my last name."

"Well of course. You are his father. I found it only fitting to do so."

Trying to find the words to cut through the uncomfortable situation but all I could come up with was "Uh, yeah."

Chapter 13

"Look I know that we have found ourselves in an awkward predicament. But both you and I are adults and we should be able to handle this as such. I don't want to make any drastic changes to your life. I just wanted to let you know and wanted to make sure you were involved."

"I get that, but what I don't get is why did you wait so long to tell me."

"I was going through my own mess. I was in shock. You have to understand. I wouldn't have in a million years thought I would be in a situation like this. Someone's "baby mama". "I know and I'm sorry. I didn't mean for this to happen either. All we can do is take care of the here and now."

We sat there and continued to talk about how we should about things from here on out. Visitation, travel and etc. Due to me already conducting business here and her being Jersey, it didn't make any sense to move. But with everything being said and arranged, I still had my doubts. Finding out would have to be handled in a delicate fashion. I knew she wouldn't do it voluntarily, I would have to get it done on my own.

Chapter 14

Traci

    I knew I was wrong for not contacting Jay in over a week. I just didn't know how to cope with his newly expressed feelings. I know that it had been a while since I had been involved with Trevor. I didn't want to make this into being some sort of rebound relationship. But instead of ghosting him, I have got to let him know how I feel and hope he understands.

    I have been a wreck this past week. I wouldn't have wished these past occurrences on my own worst enemy. I had to make an emergency visit to Dallas to check on my mom. My aunt and uncle had notified me that they were concerned they had spoken to her in awhile. And to add insult to injury, when she hadn't been answering the door when they made an appearance at her house. I knew what that meant. After a lifetime of being clean, she had to be using again. As if I needed this in my life right now. But the thing about addicts, they never pick a time

Chapter 14

that is convenient for you, it's always about them.

I arrived at DFW airport just a little afternoon. I grabbed my bags and took an Uber to my mother's house. I hadn't stepped foot in this city since leaving my mom to live with my aunt and uncle since the last time she relapsed when I was younger. When I pulled up to the house, I noticed it looked far different from what it did last time I remembered it. It was rundown. The paint on the siding of the house was starting to chip, some panels were missing. The yard was out of control and began to be overrun by overgrown weeds and dandelions. It was an absolute mess. I knew there had to be a problem. Since her recovery, it had always been something that she took pride in. She had learned how to garden when she did her last bout with recovery. It was something that took her mind off of using, so what happened?

I used my key to pry open the door. It was like it hadn't been opened in weeks, maybe evening months. The sight made me wish that I would have just stayed in L.A. Trash was all over the place and the smell, was horrid. As I continued to walk through the house the smell intensified. And I swore it was burning the insides of my nose. I opened the windows and blinds to bring some sort of light and

fresh air to the place. In the kitchen, dishes clutter the sink. Leftover food was on the tables. Even with walking through all of this, I still hadn't laid eyes on my mother.

As I continued to search, I heard a commotion coming from upstairs. I should have called someone to be there with me but I didn't. I grabbed a knife from the kitchen and proceeded to make my way up the stairs. Without waiting to make any unnecessary cause of startle or excitement, I peeked to see what was going on. I didn't want to call out for her, I was too afraid that it might have been her. And I would be announcing myself being there to an unknown stranger.

I peered into every room, when I finally came across the bedroom with her laying across the bed. Sprawled out, with the needle still in her arm. I fell to my knees. I already knew, but I tried to fight the thoughts that lead me to the conclusion. She was gone.

My mother and I might not have been close after all this time but I never thought coming back I would have caught her like this. Right at the moment I wished Jay was here. To console me, in a way that I knew that only he could.

I had to call him. After I called the police and they came and picked up her body, notified my aunt and uncles as to what happened, I called him. Regardless of the time that had passed, I had. The phone rang repeatedly, for what had seemed an eternity. I was gonna tell him, tell him everything. Let him know that I was sorry, I didn't mean to ghost him, the feelings that I had for him were the same. That I was just confused; I didn't want to hurt him or get hurt in the process. He was the only one I wanted at this moment. I needed him.

"Hello?" He answered on the final ring, right before the voicemail was about to chime. And with all that thought going through my head, the only words that came out of my mouth were, "She's gone." Why was there always a movement of vulnerability between us when we were dealing with the passing of a loved one?

Jay

I looked at the phone in complete shock. It was a call I didn't expect to ever receive. At the moment I could care less as to why I hadn't talked to her in awhile. I was just glad to hear her voice, to know that she was ok. Given the circumstance, I knew

Chapter 14

that she wasn't.

"I'm so sorry…my mother…she… in the house…I found her….Oh my God!!!"

She rambled, trying to get out the words in the midst of her constant sobs. Me on the other end trying to decipher exactly what was going on. "Sorry baby, take your time and tell me what happened." "I'm sorry. I'm so sorry. I didn't mean to call you like this after not talking to you for so long. A lot has happened since we met, and I was just confused. Everything was happening so fast. I didn't want to make it seem like you were just a rebound relationship. I didn't want you to be one. All the time that we spent together, I enjoyed every bit of it. More than I have ever with anyone I had ever been in a relationship with. I'm so sorry to call you like this but you were the only one I wanted to talk to at the moment. The only one who would know exactly how I'm feeling right now. Given you went through the same thing, I'm going through right now."

That was a mouth full. "What is it that you're going through? Who's gone?"

"My Mother. I found her in the house. She OD'ed."

My mouth dropped to the floor. After losing my mother just recently I knew exactly how she felt. I felt sorry for her. No one should have to go through what she's going through right now, finding her the way that she did. Especially not alone.

"I'm sorry, Traci. Is there anything that you want me to do?"

"No, I just know that when I'm finished with all the things I need to take care of here, when I get home I just want to be with you. I don't want to waste another moment wondering about the what if's and care about what people are going to think. I love you and I want to spend my life with you."

It was the response I had been waiting for what seemed like

forever. I knew I wanted to be with her since the first time we were together. And she finally sees that we were meant to be, she needed me. And I wasn't going to let another moment pass without being with her.

Even though Angela was still visiting, it seemed like the least of my worries. She would be enjoying her stay and I would have to catch her on the next trip. I booked my flight and I was on the first thing smoking. Headed to Dallas, to be with her.

As soon as I arrived at DFW, I was on the phone with Nat trying to find out exactly where she was staying. I let her know that it was supposed to be a surprise and to not let her know. She agreed and I was on my way. Traci was staying at a local Marriott. One that was close to the funeral home, where she needed to make all of the arrangements for her mother.

It was a quarter to 1 in the morning when I made my way to the hotel. I knew she would probably be sleepy but I just had to let her know that I was here. I took the elevator up to Room 325 and knocked on the door. I could hear the movement from behind the door, maybe she wasn't sleeping after all.

From the otherside of the door she called out, "Who is it?"

I replied, "It's Me." At that moment I knew she couldn't know who I was and all she could see through the peephole was a bouquet of roses that I purposely covered the front of my face with. I wanted to make sure I didn't miss out on the face she made when she saw that it was me, standing there in the flesh.

She opened the door in frustration, "Now it's too late and I'm too tired for people to be playing at my damn door—" She stumbled back, catching her balance when she realized it was me.

"Hey, baby. Miss me."

"How did you...when did you..."

Chapter 14

"I love the fact that I can always leave you speechless."

"You do it to me all the time."

And before I could say another word, she hopped up on me, wrapping her legs around my waist. Pulling every word from my mouth with her tongue as they intertwined. Damn, I missed her. I missed this. The way she felt, I almost exploded right then and there. But I held my composure, wanting to fill her all with the love that waited.

Traci

He carried me over to the bed, and gently placed me at the foot of it. He stood there, as I basked in all of his fineness. Damn … he was so fine, like fine, fine. It was almost as if I was seeing him for the first time. As he stood in front of me, I took that time to relieve him of his pants. Without hesitation, I unbuckled and unbuttoned them, revealing an erection that I knew was already happy to see me as well. Licking my lips and catching a glimpse of his eyes on me, I took him into my hand and massaged his growth before taking him into my mouth.

Wrapping my lips around the head and creating a suction with the inside of my mouth and lips. My eyes remained on him as he threw his head back. Within a moment Jay's hands had made their way to the back of my head, guiding me to take him deeper. He was on the verge of losing control and roared, "Fuucckk."

I smiled on the inside, because I was handling my business. He squirmed trying to keep it together as I swirled my tongue around him and maneuvered up and down his girth. Within minutes he moved back, relieving himself from my mouth. Looking at me with sex crazed eyes and said, "Next."

Shit what have I done?

It was too late to make any last minute gestures or moves. In a split second he laid me back on the bed, with my panties and sweats off as he began devouring me with his tongue. I closed my eyes as his tongue swam in my wetness, and his fingers massaged me from the inside. Trying hard not to scream as I reached my peak.

I should have known Jay was just getting started. He kissed me from my waist to my breasts and eventually Jay reached my mouth. After he kissed me and our tongues danced, he slid his fingers away from my love and licked them as if they were popsicles.

"Nasty Ass," I shot at him.

"Only for you," he assured me.

"Better be!"

I guided my hand between us and I reached for his shaft, to fill my treasure. I shuttered, as if this was our first time. Technically, it did feel like the first time. This time was more intense, more everything. He took his time and inched all of him inside of me, plunging deep inside me with every stroke.

Unable to contain myself or my screams, as my wall began to clench. I let out a yell, " Oh, Shit, Baby. Ahh, Joseph."

"Yes baby. Say my name."

"Jooseppphhhh"

"That's right, baby. Fuckkkkkk!"

We climaxed in unison and held each other tightly, taking in our special moment.

* * *

He couldn't have come at a better time, both literally and figuratively. It was exactly what the doctor ordered. And I

Chapter 14

couldn't have thanked him enough. He helped me get through it all. He assisted with the funeral arrangements and the repass. Nat, my uncle and my aunt as well. Good thing that when she first got clean, I procured a life insurance policy for her so everything was covered. Plus more. I don't know what I would have done without that. Hell I don't know what I would have done without any of them.

The funeral service was lovely. The funeral director dressed her in her favorite yellow dress with her tan heels. Her hair was laid for the gods. Even in her resting state she was beautiful. "I'm going to miss you mama," I said as I passed the casket and gently kissed her on her forehead. Even though me and her had our ups and down, she was the only mama I knew and the only one I would ever have. She always wanted the best for me, and even from above, I will continue to make her proud.

As I made my way to my seat, I couldn't help but glance over the crowd. There were so many people in attendance. Mrs. Sharlene and her husband, Mr. Wilt, Mr. Carl from the convenience store down the street and so many others came to pay their respects. It warmed my heart to see all the people who cared to show up. She was always active in the church even though she had a constant battle with her own demons. Hell, we all did.

Taking my seat, I couldn't help but notice Trevor was also in attendance.

What the hell was he doing here?

Not only did he have the audacity to show up, but he brought his girl ... his pregnant girl. I was too done! After I'd taken the time to process Trevor and his family were present, I was ready to go home and be far away from Trevor's drama. I'm so done. At this point, I couldn't wait to be done with this and be back at home drama free.

At the repass, Trevor couldn't leave well enough alone, and had to make his presence known and show his ass simultaneously. He walked over to me. Thankfully, he had the good sense to leave his plus one behind.

"Hey there, Beautiful. Sorry to hear about your mom. She was a great woman."

"Thank you." Were the only sounds I was able to release through my clenched teeth. I used my better judgment and refrained from doing something that would bring disgrace to myself or my family.

"Hey, I just wanted to let you know that I was sorry. Sorry for everything that went down between us. I'm just sorry."

Sorry, he was damn right he was sorry. Sorry for wasting my time, sorry for wasting my love, just plain sorry. "Coming from you, I would say thank you and I forgive you. But I could really care less. You thought that I would give you some kind of pity or whatever you were thinking because you showed up at my mother's funeral. Well, I don't know what the hell you thought. And also I'm guessing that you are starting to see the error of your ways by coming up to me apologizing. You must be realizing that you got seventy/thirty. You had you a good woman. Now what you got. Probably nothing. I can't say that I feel sorry for you or anything. But you know what I forgive you. Because if it wasn't for you letting me see how much a no good son of a bitch you were when you did. I wouldn't have found the good man that I have now. So Thank you Trevor and I hope you have a good life with your girl and your new baby."

"Everything alright over here," Jay said as he inserted himself into the conversation. "Yeah, everything is fine. We're done here." placing my arm inside of his as we walked away. The

Chapter 14

first sign of calm in a while. Glad it was all over.

Chapter 15

Jay

We made it back home, safely. Traci decided that she wanted to stay with me, while on break from the company. Not only that but we wanted to make up for lost time. I called off from work as well. We spent every waking moment in bed, naked, sex tangled. It was nice. I woke up to her beautiful face every morning.

"What would you like to do today?" she yawned as she stretched her arms out and stood up in the bed.

"As long as I'm next to you, it really doesn't matter."

"We can't spend forever in this bed, we have to do something."

"Speak for yourself," I said as I reached for the covers and placed them back over me. "I know you're probably hungry. At least we can go out to eat or something."

"You know what, that sounds perfect!"

"Alright then. Let me just hop in the shower. We can leave

Chapter 15

when I get out."

I knew it had to have been only a couple of minutes while I was in the shower. I heard a knock, voices, a little movement, and when I grabbed my towel to get out she was gone. A note with the paternity test results were on the table. The note said, "Checkmate, MotherFucker." Fuck!

That night when I left to go to Dallas, I knew I left abruptly. I didn't tell Angela until after I left. Messed up, I know. It was an emergency! The women that I loved needed me. I told Angela that it was a family emergency and I needed to fly out that night. That was all she needed to know. I apologize for any inconvenience and told her if she wanted to stay, I would accommodate her. If she wanted to leave, that would be cool as well. I would just hit her up when I returned. Who would have known at the point that the time I would have stayed out there would have been over a week? It wasn't like I planned it. Just like the pregnancy it just happened, she should understand, right. Let me not be a dick about, cause I'm far from that. Regardless of the situation, I never meant for it to go down like that.

Traci

I can't believe it. Traci, you just attract these nothing ass negros. You ain't pregnant, don't have any kids but you attract all the negros that got babies. Is there a stamp on my forehead that says accepting men and their baby's mama? I never wanted that drama. That wasn't what I signed up for. I just wanted to be happy with a man who loved me. Now was that too much to ask. I think not.

"Your life should be a movie girl! How you end up with two men with Hocus Pocus ass baby mama's. Where'd that bitch come from anyway?" Nat asked, grabbing her popcorn and sitting next to me on the couch.

"I don't know she just showed up, asking for Joseph. With a baby in tow. I told her that he was in the shower right now, may I ask who she was? Told me her name was Angela, the mother of his child. Why didn't he even tell me? That baby was new new, you hear me. Had to have just been born. Nat, why didn't he just tell me? He knew about everything with my ex, then my mom. I just can't anymore heartbreak. This year has done me in. I just want to curl up, lay here and stay here."

"Well, you know you can't stay here forever. We still have a business to run. But I know you're going through a lot right now. So I'm going to let you wallow in your self pity. But only for a little while, ok? I know there has to be a reasonable explanation for everything. He loves you. I know he does. He's already shown that he does, countless times. You can't just throw it all away like that. He is totally different from Trevor, so you can't cast him in that pond as of yet.

I laid there and shrugged off what she just said. Reasonable explanation my ass. If he would have told me in the first place there wouldn't have been a need to explain. These negros and their secrets. Didn't they mama's ever tell them that what's done in the dark always comes to the light. I know mine did. Foolishness.

At that moment, my phone rang. I already knew who it was. I smoothed my hand over my face and massaged my temples. I already could feel a slight headache coming on. Jay had been calling me ever since I left his house. I'm pretty sure I had a ton of messages of him telling me that he was sorry, the whole song and dance. I knew all about it. I can't, I just couldn't right now.

Jay

Chapter 15

I rushed over to the hotel where Angela was staying and knocked on the door. She opened it with such a smug ass look on her face, knowing that it would have been me coming to address the situation. On the way over I already knew I was 38 hot. But I had to calm myself down, in order to make sure that I didn't cause a scene. I just needed this all to be over and done with. So I could move on and get to the next chapter of my life.

Without saying a word, I barged into the room.

"Well hello to you too." she said as I passed her and stood.

"Now ain't the time for casualties, why did you even show up at my house? I explained everything to you in the letter that I sent to you. I told you I had my doubts from the beginning. I knew I wasn't the child's father. And I think deep down you knew it as well. Why would you even try to continue on with this charade."

"You didn't know until after the test came. And why are you trying to play me? Had me waiting here, while you were off with that bitch. Family emergency my ass. Me showing up there was exactly what you get. Did you think your little test was going to dismiss me anyway? My baby still has your last name, so you're going to have to pay regardless."

Trying to refrain from calling her out of her name, "So this what it was all about? Your baby's daddy was a broke nigga from Jersey and given that I gave you just a sliver of an opportunity to be with someone above your low ass standards, you wanted to try and trap me? You females are a trip nowadays. Listen, you have until tomorrow morning to grab you and your baby's shit and be up out of this room. After that the charges are all on you. I'll be letting the hotel know of the current situation, so if you try anything stupid you will be charged for that as well. And if you care to take this any further, I promise you that I will make sure this decision is something that you live to regret. I will be sending you the papers as well for you to have the baby's last name changed as well. I hope you have a nice life Angela. Take care, and take care little man."

And I left, leaving her stuck. We've always heard the tales about men being caught up in those kinds of situations, but it wasn't going to be me. Not today, not ever. Now I had to figure out how to get my woman back. I just got her, I wasn't going to lose her. Not like this.

***

I've sent flowers, chocolates, edible arrangements and more trying to get her to at least talk to me. I know I messed up. I should have told her, I know. Damn! I didn't know what else to do. Nat just told me she needed time and eventually she would come around. So time was what I gave her. It had been a whole month. I swear we spent more time apart than exactly in a relationship. I never understood why this had to be so hard. I guess once you find the one you're destined for, you have to go through a couple of loops. To make sure that once it completely locked down you would appreciate it more. And she was my destiny, I knew it. There was only one thing left to do and hopefully it would work.

Traci

Sometime had past, I had to get back to my normal self. Even though I felt far from it. Business still had to be taken care of. I decided that instead of staying in the house and reminding myself of my past failures, I would bury myself in work. I wanted to try and take my mind off of things, but it was hard

Chapter 15

when there was a constant reminder of him everywhere. He had sent flowers to my house, my job.

"Now you know that man loves you, when are you at least going to hear him out?" Nat asked springing into my office and handing me a bunch of mail.

"I can't with that right now. What do we have on the schedule for today?" I replied, as I shuffled through the stack of wasted paper and junk.

"We have a meeting at 5, with the employees to talk about upcoming events and contracts to talk over for finalizations. And that will be about it for the day. How are you going to ask me a question and not pay attention to what I'm saying? What are you looking at?" Nat said puzzled. "It's a paternity test. From Jay. It says the baby isn't his." My mouth hung open. "What the hell have I done. I didn't even let him explain. Instead, I just reacted. How could he forgive me for this? He's been trying to love me since the beginning and all I've done was push him away. Nat what am I supposed to do now."

"Girl, What do you mean what do you do now? You go and get your man!"

"What about the meeting?"

"What about it? That's why you have a partner. I got this. Wouldn't be the first meeting you've missed and I'm damn sure it probably won't be the last. Go and handle your business, Traci." Nat was already grabbing my things and pushing me toward the door.

Just as I made my way down to the lobby, there he was ... as if he was waiting for me to arrive, almost as if he planned on meeting me there. I looked in Nat's direction and squinted my eyes at her. I knew she had something to do with this, but I was grateful.

Walking up to him, my face said it all. "I'm sorry for not letting you explain—" the words couldn't even get out of my mouth fast enough before he had my face in his hand bringing it in to gently kiss me on my lips.

"No need." That was all he said before he began kissing me again.

Love had interrupted, my thoughts ... my plans ... my everything.

But it was all worth it. He was worth it. Fate had written a perfect story, and I couldn't have picked a happier ending.

About the Author

Dria Bond is an avid reader turned author. She believes in the quote of Toni Morrison, *"If there is a book that you want to read, but it hasn't been written yet, you must be the one to write it."* *So she took it and ran with it. Dria Bond is also a proud wife, mother, and entrepreneur, who resides in Texas.*

You can connect with me on:
- https://www.blackbirdbooksdfw.com
- https://www.facebook.com/BlackbirdBooksDFW

Made in United States
North Haven, CT
18 June 2024